I0788589

# BREAKING THE SUUN

## LEGENDS OF THE FALLEN BOOK 5

J.A. CULICAN

CASSIDY TAYLOR

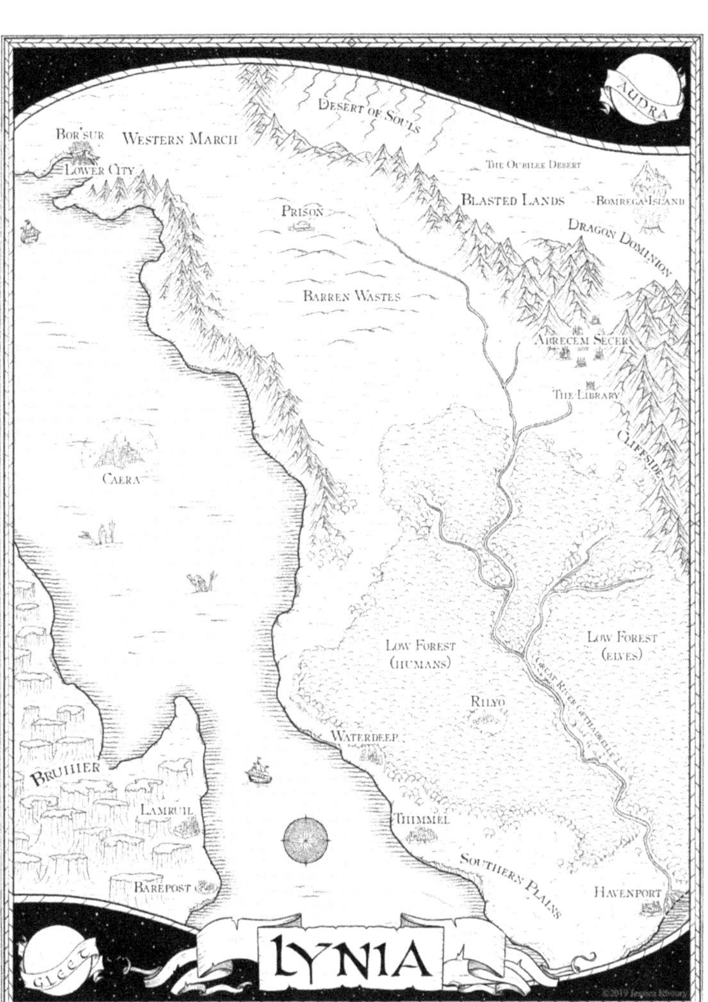

AUDRA
DESERT OF SOULS
BOR'SUR
WESTERN MARCH
THE OUBILEE DESERT
LOWER CITY
BLASTED LANDS
BOMREGA ISLAND
PRISON
DRAGON DOMINION
BARREN WASTES
AIRECEM SECER
THE LIBRARY
CAERA
CLIFFSIDE
LOW FOREST
(HUMANS)
LOW FOREST
(ELVES)
RILYO
WATERDEEP
BRUHIER
THIMMEL
LAMRUIL
SOUTHERN PLAINS
BAREPOST
HAVENPORT
GLEET
LYNIA
GREAT RIVER GETHAURELL
©2019 Jessica Khoury

# CHAPTER 1

I felt like I'd been holding my breath for three years without even knowing it. The farther away the *Iron Duchess* flew from Barepost the lighter I felt, and not just because we were flying, though that certainly didn't hurt.

"Do you feel it too?" I asked Stiarna. We perched on the main mast's yardarm, the sail billowing out and rippling beneath us. This had become our favorite place on the entire ship these last couple days. When Arun didn't have us swabbing decks, or running around tying down ropes and sails, this was where we were.

She blinked at me, and then turned her face back into the wind. It ruffled the brown feathers at her neck. She made a happy clucking sound I thought was as close to an agreement as I would get from her.

"Frida!" Arun called from below, where he stood with both hands on the wheel. The elf looked right at home, his hair wind-blown, and his cheeks ruddy from being in the sun so long. He dressed in a light tunic and linen pants rolled just past his ankles and belted at the waist. His feet were bare. He didn't look like a gentry elf or a miner anymore. He looked like a sailor. Like a captain. "Look." He pointed straight ahead.

I pulled myself to my feet, holding to the rigging for balance, and shaded my eyes with my hand to look where he was pointing. In the distance, a small plateau rose out of the veil, like a fish sticking its head out of water. Instead of the usual tangle of untamed forest, though, this plateau seemed to be someone's home. Except for a small grove on the northernmost edge, most of the trees had been cleared and the plateau's top was a large, intricate garden. There were colorful bushes and flowers, large stone fountains, and a winding hedge maze. In the middle was a large stone building. Best of all? There wasn't a monster in sight.

I climbed down the rigging, Stiarna leaping gracefully after me. The wing which had been injured by the ur'gel was still bound to her side, but it did not seem to hinder her catlike agility. I knew she longed to fly, though. I thought that was why she sat those long hours on the yardarm with me. Up there, I could almost believe we were flying again, just the two of us as we had that once. It was the only other time in recent memory I could remember feeling carefree.

"Is that the temple?" I asked Arun, coming to stand beside him. We were the only ones on deck, the others preferring to spend their time mostly in the crew's quarters or the galley, a few of them looking a little green around the gills. Especially my big brother, Erik.

"This is it," he confirmed.

The pale stone structure on the plateau was tall with dozens of domed towers clustered together. Instead of thatching, though, the roof was made of some type of red metal that reflected the sun. Arun turned the ship. The sunlight flashed brightly, seeming to follow us as we moved in our slow circle. He pushed on the lever beside the wheel and we began to descend, aiming right for the center of the garden.

"Are we landing?" Grissall asked as she and Xalph emerged

from the crew's quarters, followed close behind by my siblings, Erik and Estrid, and the spare adventurers we had picked up on the way out of Barepost—Beru and Aria. They gathered by the railing, looking down.

A woman emerged from the temple, her hand over her eyes as she watched us. She seemed to glow, her orange gown sparkling as she moved, hair covered by a matching hood. Her neck and fingers were adorned with golden jewelry I could see even at this distance, but it didn't seem pretentious like it did on Stephan Luthair, Governor of Barepost. It seemed, instead, to be a mere part of her persona. As though she would be incomplete without it.

"Da would never believe this," Xalph said, leaning far over the edge.

I put my hand on his shoulder, drawing him back. His dad was Haklang, the foreman of the Barepost mine, and he'd only let Arun escape if we promised to take Xalph with us. He'd grown up in the mines, even been crushed in a cave-in that crippled one of his legs and took an eye. Having spent the first ten years of his life underground, he saw everything with new eyes and loved every bit of it.

"Who is that?" Grissall asked. She was the daughter of the innkeeper, Gerves, who had taken pity on us and let us live at his inn for three years while we scraped out a living on Barepost. Even though she was several years older, she and Xalph had become fast friends, bonding as the youngest members of our crew.

"The priest," Erik answered. "She serves the light."

"Lunla," Aria supplied. She and Beru had spent time here before, which was why they'd chosen to consult with this priest about my identity.

"And the ur'gels?" Xalph asked. "They serve the dark?"

"I think that's safe to assume," my brother conceded.

Far enough away I couldn't hear what they were saying, Aria

and Beru talked excitedly to each other. It reminded me why we were here, and my stomach tightened with anxiety. I touched the mark beside my eye. The five-pointed star Beru had called the mark of Onen Suun. He believed because of it, I was destined to save the world. I hoped this priest of light would be able to tell him—and everyone else—otherwise.

Eventually, Arun ordered us away from the railing and began barking orders to prepare us for landing. Half of what he said—or maybe more—I didn't understand, but I tried to do my best, adjusting sails and rudders as directed. The ship lurched to a stop, rocking perilously before settling with a groan in the middle of the temple's garden.

Stiarna was the first off the ship, leaping over the side and disappearing into the shrubbery, likely heading toward the grove we'd seen from the sky in search of small prey. Arun and Erik lowered the gangplank and guided the other passengers off the ship. When I passed Erik he gripped my hand, looking like he wanted to say something, but then he released me, and I continued down the walkway. I knew he was angry with me, but I could only hope he would be able to forgive me. Maybe once this was over, once we were en route to our home in Bor'-sur, he would realize that what I'd done to get us out of Bare-post had been necessary. That the choices I'd been given were not choices at all.

It was nice to be back on solid ground. The grass was soft beneath my feet, the air smelled sweet and earthy. The priest stood in front of us, arms crossed as she took stock of us, waiting until Erik and Arun had joined us to speak.

"I am Lunla." She crossed a hand over her chest and lowered her head in a small bow. "Priest of light, and warden of this temple. I welcome you to this blessed place, familiar friends and strangers." She beckoned us to follow her, so we did, trailing behind her in a straight line like ducklings, up the stairs and into the temple.

Past the foyer, we found ourselves in what seemed to be some kind of grand meeting room. The ceilings arched high overhead, supported by thick stone columns, rows of benches faced away from us, and at the front of the room was a raised dais. Behind the dais, an altar squatted in front of a massive, floor-to-ceiling glass window. These windows lined the walls on either side. Each of them was stained a different color, so the room was cast in colorful lights.

It made complete sense to me why someone might choose to serve the light, as lovely as it was in that moment.

Xalph was obviously taken by it, immediately setting off to explore with Grissall on his heels.

Lunla stopped halfway into the room and turned back to us, tucking her hands inside her sleeves. "Tell me, how may I serve you?" she asked politely.

Beru pulled me forward from where I'd been lingering in the back of the group, my face turned toward the stone ceiling, studying the intricate carvings there. I stumbled a bit over my own two feet, but Beru caught me, standing me upright in front of the priest. She looked at me with polite disinterest, her lips pressed into a dull smile, then turned back to Beru. He still had one hand wrapped tightly around my upper arm. I would have shaken him off, but I was too nervous to do even that.

"I believe I have found Onen Suun's heir, the key to saving the world from the Dark."

Lunla watched Beru for another long second, and just as he opened his mouth to speak, she held up a hand. As if from nowhere, two younger women, girls really, dressed in the orange robes of the priests, appeared. "Girls," Lunla said without turning to look at them. "Please, show our guests the gardens. I would like to have a word in private with Sir Beru."

Relieved, I turned to follow Erik and the rest, but stopped when Lunla added, "And his Suun heir."

Erik glanced back once, but I nodded at him, letting him

know it was fine. It was probably better to get this over with anyway. They left through a small side door which clicked quietly behind them, leaving the three of us alone in the cavernous room.

When he couldn't stand the silence anymore, Beru spoke quickly, "I recognize her by the star beside her eye. As you know, Onen Suun had the same mark, a blessing from the Creator."

"Hmm." Lunla made the noise low in her throat, and I couldn't tell if it was a noise of disbelief, disapproval, or maybe even agreement. Finally, she turned her gaze to the mark beside my eye.

I stood uncomfortably, waiting for her verdict.

But she did not respond right away. Instead, she turned away and walked toward the front of the room. It was fair to say she glided rather than walked, her footsteps light and silent. Beru and I, on the other hand, clomped behind her, our boots thudding against the stone floor. A nondescript girl who had been tending the altar behind the dais peeked over her shoulder, saw us coming, and darted away, disappearing through some other hidden doorway. The place made me uneasy, with all its secret passages.

On the altar was a glass bowl of clear water reflecting light onto the ceiling, and on the other side, a metal bowl of smoldering embers glowing subtly orange. Lunla took an iron poker and stoked the coals, sparks jumping and crackling.

Without turning back to us, she said, "The light comes to us in many different forms." She went to the water, dipped in the two fingers of her right hand, and touched them to her forehead before turning back around.

I wished she'd hurry up.

"Two hundred years ago, it came to us in the form of a man called Onen Suun. His light extinguished the dark, but the darkness is emerging once again." She turned to look at Beru, ignoring me completely. "Sir Beru, just as last time, you will have an important role to play in what is coming, but you should not look to this girl for your answers."

My shoulders slumped with relief, but only until I'd processed her words. She had not said I wasn't the Suun heir, just that it was none of Beru's concern.

Beru seemed to realize this, too. "I don't know what else to do. The Light Woman was a dead end. I bring you the Suun heir and you tell me I'm looking in the wrong place. I don't know where to go from here."

Lunla raised her eyebrows. "I did not say you were looking in the wrong place. But perhaps you are searching for the wrong thing."

Beru opened his mouth to continue but the priest held up two fingers again, and the small girl we'd seen earlier reappeared, a broom in her hand.

"Please escort Sir Beru and his companion, Aria, into town so that they may continue their quest elsewhere."

"And the others?" Beru asked, looking from her, to me, and then back again.

I was just as confused as he was.

Lunla clasped her hands in front of her, her orange sleeves draping over her wrists and nearly brushing the dark red rug on the floor. She smiled serenely at Beru, as a mother might indulge a curious child. "Do not worry for them. You came into each other's lives when it was necessary. Here is where your paths diverge."

"This way," said the girl, opening a door and gesturing for Beru to follow.

After a small hesitation, he did, without a glance back at me.

When the door had closed behind them, Lunla turned back to the altar and lowered her head as if in contemplation. A rainbow of colored light—red and orange and green—fell across her shoulders.

I didn't dare speak or move. I barely even breathed. It wasn't so much that I didn't want to disturb her as it was I didn't want her to remember I was there. I didn't want her to turn her attention to me and say something reinforcing Beru's idea I was the Suun heir, because I knew deep down in my bones I wasn't. I couldn't be. And I didn't know how to tell a priest she was wrong.

It wasn't long, though, before she broke the silence. "Your journey also does not end here." She turned from the altar and moved past me to sit on the front bench, her legs crossed primly at the ankles. She didn't invite me to join her.

"I never thought it did," I told her.

"But it also is not yet over. If I may give you one piece of advice, it would be this: open your mind. Be prepared for what you might find. That it might be unexpected. That your role in this might be greater than you intend. But the unexpected is not always bad."

For me, it almost always had been. "Am I the Suun heir, though?"

Luna sighed, for the first time looking a little tired, her serene mask dropping. "Unfortunately, that information is not in my realm of knowledge. But, if I were the one steering this destiny, I would not be so quick to label any one person the savior of the world."

It reminded me of what Arun had said to me a few days ago before we'd left the plateau above Barepost. That no one could get by without a little help. Maybe she was right and Onen Suun's legacy didn't lie with any one of us, but with all of us.

In which case, we were fairly certainly doomed.

# CHAPTER 2

I batted Erik's sword away with my own and thrust forward once, twice, three times, before driving the blade home, stopping a breath from his chest.

He grumbled and stepped away, throwing his sword to the ground.

"You must fight through the pain," Estrid insisted, but Erik wasn't listening.

He was pacing, rubbing his arm through the white linen bandage and grimacing at the touch. He'd been burned in the galestone explosion, and then used the arm to fight off Luthair's men on the plateau. Aria told him the damage to the nerves might be permanent and he would just have to work through the pain or let it rest. Erik did not believe in rest.

"Don't be so hard on him," I snapped at her.

"He's going to have to learn."

"And he will. Give him time."

She bared her teeth at me, brushing a strand of hair back from her face. One of the girls had shaved one side of it for her last night, but she'd left the other side long. Instead of making her look lopsided, she looked even fiercer than before. "Want to fight someone your own size?" she quipped, a joke we often tossed back and forth at each other, both of us being smaller than Erik.

I spread my arms, sword in one hand, ax in the other, welcoming her. She bounced off the stone wall where she'd been sitting and crossed the grass, a short sword in each hand. Erik was the only one of us who fought with a shield, and only because he was big enough to use it as a weapon. Even though Estrid and I were larger than the average human woman—and even the average human male—we both found a shield too burdensome. Though we'd seen Erik smash in enough faces with it to understand its purpose.

Estrid wasted no more time posturing. She came at me in a whirl of blades, but I knew all her tricks. I'd been watching her and Erik train since before I ever picked up a weapon. I still remembered the chilly winter mornings on the cliff, perched in the twisted branches of a live oak tree while they sparred back and forth below me, each pushing the other closer and closer to the edge. My heart had always been in my throat, watching them in their intricate, dangerous dance. When I was finally old enough to join them, neither of them had ever pushed me as hard or as far as they did each other. It had made me work even harder to prove myself to them. I felt like, in a way, I was still trying.

I knocked Estrid's swords away, one after the other, and spun, coming in low. It was her weakness—she liked to go high. But she didn't let me in, dancing away easily, avoiding the reach of my blades. We were in the courtyard between the temple and the hedge maze, alone except for a few of the priest's maids tending the garden. They were watching us surreptitiously, having not quite mastered the art of indifference their mistress had.

Stiarna, who had disappeared all night, sat on a distant crumbling stone wall sunning herself. Arun was doing some repairs on the *Iron Duchess*, while Xalph and Grissall played in the maze. Their shouts and laughter were the only sounds in the entire world other than the clashing of our blades.

We were evenly matched, both of us fast and ruthless. Every lunge met with a block. Every step met with another. Erik had grown bored and was practicing on his own, ignoring us as he battled an invisible opponent. The sun was rising higher in the sky, and there was no shade except for that cast by the temple's towers. Sweat dripped into my eyes and made my hands slick, but I hadn't been this happy in a long time.

She was testing my left side, the side that had been injured by the ur'gel in the attack on Barepost. Her attacks came one after the other, and I deflected all of them with the ax in my left hand. My shoulder ached, and my hand burned. I spun, trying to move her to my right, but she just went with me, relentlessly trying to prove her point. That we would just have to fight through the pain. Live with it. Deal with it. Use it.

But even Estrid was wearing out. One sloppy swing was all it took, and I was on the offensive again, driving her back toward the entrance to the hedge maze. I went low, and even though she was expecting it this time, she wasn't expecting my foot to lash out and sweep her feet out from under her. She landed on her hip but didn't pause, her own feet scissoring around my ankles and jerking me down.

We collapsed onto the ground, side by side, laughing and panting, the grass hot against my back and the sun bright enough I had to close my eyes.

Erik came over and nudged me with his boot.

I squinted up at his silhouette.

"Are you going to tell us what the priest told you?" he asked.

"Vague ramblings you might expect from a priest."

"But are you … the heir?" He sat beside me and stretched his long legs out in front of him.

I kept my eyes on his boots instead of his face. "No."

Estrid pushed herself onto her elbows. "She said no? Thank Onen, I knew it but—"

"Not exactly," I said. "Just that he shouldn't count on me."

She collapsed back onto the ground, laughing.

On my other side, Erik snickered. "I thought she would at least tell us something we didn't already know."

"You guys are very funny." I pushed myself up until I was sitting and hugged my knees to my chest.

"Oh, Frida." Erik put an arm around my shoulders and pulled me tight against him in a half-hug. "You didn't think it was true, did you?"

I fought against him, pushing myself back upright and off his shoulder. "Well, no," I admitted, "but it is weird, right?"

"What's weird?" Estrid asked. "That someone would think you're Onen Suun's heir?"

I pulled a face at her over my shoulder. "The mark. That Onen Suun had the same one and was supposed to pass it on to his descendants. Is it just a coincidence?"

"If it were the mark of Onen Suun, wouldn't your mother have had it, too?"

"You're sure she didn't?"

Estrid nodded, no longer joking. "She didn't. She was a normal woman. Kind, beautiful, smart, but normal."

Kind, beautiful, and smart enough to leave me, her daughter, when I was just three years old. "What did you think when the mark appeared?"

"At first it just looked like dirt."

Erik nudged my back. "You were a *very* dirty child."

I rolled my eyes at him.

Estrid continued, "I remember I couldn't keep you still enough to wipe it off, so I just thought it was dirt for the longest time. But instead of fading or washing off in the bath, it just got darker and more defined. When I finally asked Father about it, he told me just what he always says—that it was a blessing from the ancestors."

I wiped my finger across the mark as if I could rub it away. "Did he ever seem sad that she left?"

Erik shrugged. "You know how Father is."

"He turned it into a learning opportunity," Estrid added, as if I needed an explanation. Father was a teacher before he was a warrior. He'd treated our upbringing as one big test. He was always asking us what we thought, what we would do, what the next steps were in any given situation. "So, even if he was sad, he didn't let us see."

"Do you think my mom knew something? Is that why she left?"

"Better yet," Erik added, "do you think Father knows something?"

Why had I never thought of that? They said my mother arrived in Bor'sur with no family and no desire to talk about her past. Our father had taken her under his protection—*Love at first sight*, he always said—and ten months later, I was born. Was it possible he had known she was a descendant of Onen Suun, and their child would be, too? But Estrid had said my mother didn't have the mark. So, was it possible, then, she'd already been pregnant when she'd come to Bor'sur? Had my father raised a stranger's child? And if so, why had she left me behind with a family that wasn't my own?

"I think he must know something," I said quietly. "But why wouldn't he tell me?"

Erik shrugged. "To spare you. To make sure you fit in."

"Well, it didn't work." I flopped back down beside Estrid, and Erik stretched out on my other side, folding his arms under his head.

"What do you mean?" Estrid asked, her eyes closed as the sun crept slowly across the garden, warming our leathers and staining our cheeks pink.

I chewed on my bottom lip before answering, giving voice to a feeling I'd always been afraid to bring up. "I've always been on the outside. There's just something you two have that I'm missing."

"That's ridiculous." Estrid swatted at me blindly.

"You're a Svand," Erik said, "no matter what anyone else says. Or doesn't say."

When I didn't respond, Estrid sat up and turned to face me. Her sword was in her lap, and she ran a slender finger along its length. "Look, Erik and I spent the first several years of our lives as just the two of us. In the selfish way of children, we never expected Father to find another wife, and we certainly didn't expect there to be another baby. So, maybe you're right. Maybe there is something between us that you don't share, like the years that it was just the two of us, but that doesn't make what you have with us any less special. Or any less real. You're our little sister, no matter who your ancestors are."

Listening to her, all I could think about was the time she and Erik had sent me into a tree to retrieve one of Father's arrows that Erik had shot into the branches and lost. They told me I was smaller and lighter and quicker. That there was no one better for the job. On the way down, my trousers had snagged on a broken branch and I hadn't been able to work them free. I'd shouted for help, but Erik—to whom I'd already thrown the arrow—had turned to Estrid.

"Do you hear anything?"

"No." She shook her head. "Just the wind."

And they'd skipped happily away, the arrow in hand. I'd stayed in that tree until nightfall when a hunter had passed below on his way back to Bor'sur and helped me down.

I was a little worried Estrid was doing the same thing to me now—saying what I wanted to hear. Keeping me complacent and happy. What would it take for me to become invisible to them? If we discovered the truth wasn't what I wanted to hear? At what point would they leave me again?

"Maybe it is just a coincidence," Erik said after a pause, "especially if the priest didn't agree with Beru."

I tried to remember exactly what it was Lunla had said. What her non-answer had been. She'd told me I would play a part in the fight that was coming. And she'd told me to be prepared for what I might find, even if what I found wasn't what I wanted or expected. I was that little girl in a tree again, chasing an arrow I couldn't see.

I only hoped when I came crashing down, Erik and Estrid would still be there to catch me.

<h1 style="text-align:center">CHAPTER 3</h1>

I swiped a finger into a sauce simmering on the stove and popped it into my mouth. It was thick and creamy, somehow both salty and sweet. Delicious.

The cook, one of the only women not wearing orange robes, swatted at me with a wooden spoon.

"Hands off," she ordered. "It's not ready yet."

The temple's kitchen had become one of my favorite places on the plateau. It was hot and crowded and loud, but it smelled divine, and all the noise kept the grim thoughts at bay. Who I was didn't matter when I was faced with the even more pressing question—what's for dinner?

"If you're going to be in here, you can at least help." The cook pounded a mound of dough into submission as she spoke, a halo of white flour around her black braids.

From her spot on a stool near the door, Estrid called, "You'll regret that. She'll burn the place down."

I glared at her. "I've told you, Gerves didn't tell me—"

The cook held up a hand. "No bickering in the kitchen. And no talking of burning places down. I'm not trying to anger Vulca when we finally have guests at the temple."

I didn't think the god of fire much cared what I did or did not burn, but I kept my opinion to myself, only because I didn't want to anger the cook.

"I meant you could fetch the others—the elf and the children. Tell them to wash for dinner."

The elf. I hadn't talked to Arun since before we'd landed. He'd known why we were coming, but he didn't yet know what Lunla had told me. *I* wasn't even sure what Lunla had told me, and I didn't really feel like rehashing it again with someone else. Even though I would be interested to hear what he had to say. He always had a unique point of view.

I left the kitchen and followed the winding stone corridor to the front of the temple. The *Iron Duchess* was docked in the front garden, her sails rolled tight. Arun balanced on the rigging high on the mainmast, replacing a piece of broken wood.

"Ahoy there," I called up to him with a smile.

He glanced down, saw me, and held up a finger. "I'll be right there."

The gangplank had been pulled back inside, so instead, I climbed the cargo nets at the hull and pulled myself over the railing.

"Try doing that when we're thousands of feet in the air." Arun dropped to the deck a few yards away. He unhooked the heavy tool belt from his waist and let it fall to the deck. He was sweating, his long, brown hair sticking to his face and neck. He pulled it back and deftly wrapped it with a length of cord.

"You know I'm always up for a challenge." I grinned at him. It felt nice to talk to him again, just the two of us. It reminded me of when we'd explored the yooperlite cavern. It had been only days ago, but it felt like a different lifetime. "What were you doing up there?" I pointed to the mainmast.

"Fixing the last yardarm," he said. "After this, the rest of the repairs will be primarily cosmetic."

"What about the sails?" There was one crumpled at my feet

that had a long tear in it. Aria had stitched it up with black thread, and while it had gotten us here, I worried it wouldn't hold to get us anywhere else we decided to go.

"Like I said—cosmetic."

I grimaced.

"You shouldn't worry so much," he said with a laugh. "Maybe you should let me teach you about her, so you'll have a better understanding of how she flies."

"That … sounds incredibly boring," I admitted. "Unless your lesson involves letting me take the wheel."

He laughed, a full-hearted sound that brought another grin to my face. "That sounds … incredibly dangerous."

"So, no?"

"Will you let me wield your ax?"

My hand automatically went to the ax-head at my waist. "Not on your life." It had nearly driven me mad when Luthair had confiscated it. I wasn't planning on parting with it ever again. At least not voluntarily.

He laughed again. "What brings you to the *Duchess*?" He asked, wiping his hands on a scrap of white cloth he then swiped across his forehead. "If you're not here to learn all you can about her, that is."

"Dinner. The cook sent me to fetch you for dinner."

He turned back to the ship and tilted his head back to look up at the mast. "I could use a break," he admitted. "But I'm not terribly hungry."

"Then you can keep me company. Have you been in the maze yet?" I was almost certain he hadn't. He'd hardly stepped off the ship since we'd arrived. It was as if he were afraid to leave her again, considering what happened last time.

"No," he confirmed.

"Come with me to find Xalph and Grissall. Maybe the walk will work up your appetite, and if I get lost, I can blame you." I grinned at him again, but when I realized I was doing it, forced myself to stop.

He lowered the gangplank to let us off the ship instead of making me climb back down. As we clambered down the wooden walkway, he stayed close to me. Close enough I could feel the whisper of his hand on the small of my back. I led him around the temple and through the garden walls in the back until finally we stood at the entrance to the hedge maze. We paused, listening. There was a small giggle and a shout from somewhere deep inside the maze.

"After you," Arun urged.

"What a gentleman." I stepped forward and followed the green walls until we came to the first fork.

"Which way?" he asked.

I shrugged. Even though I'd seen the general shape of the maze from above in the airship, I couldn't recall any specifics about the paths. "Right," I said finally. "It has to lead to the center eventually, right?"

Arun laughed. "Sure."

We walked in silence for a time, trying and failing to follow the sounds of Grissall's giggles and Xalph's shouts. They seemed to come from all around us, but never grew any closer.

"So," Arun said eventually, "are you the Suun heir?"

I tilted my head from side to side considering. "It's still up for debate."

"You mean the priest wasn't clear? Shocking."

We reached another division, this one with three paths.

I turned to him. "Your turn."

He studied the three paths. They all looked the same. Finally, he motioned to the one on the right.

As we walked, I told him about what Lunla had said and how confused I was by the whole situation. "I know I'm not a descendant of Onen Suun. I just don't know why the priest would lead me on like this."

"Words can be powerful," Arun said. "Imagine if a single yes or no from you could change the course of someone's life. And how that change might impact the fate of the world."

He was in the lead now, and I studied his back. The way his muscles shifted beneath his light shirt. The way his hand kept coming up to rub the back of his neck. A nervous habit, maybe? When he looked back at me, I offered him a small, grim smile.

"I guess I would just like that confirmation that I am who I've always tried to be." I had never fit in and finding out I had this whole other destiny, something my brother and sister would never have to face. Something that would set me even further apart from them. What would that do to us? Where would that leave me?

Ahead of us, the maze divided again. I stood on my tiptoes to try to see over the top of the hedge, but all I could see were rows and rows of green with no distinguishable paths. The temple was to our right, so unless we had passed the center...

"This way," I said, motioning to the left.

"I thought we were going to the right."

"Yeah, well, plans change."

We took another left, a right, another right, ran into a dead end and backtracked. I lost track eventually but kept the temple always at our backs, if possible, until we finally emerged into what had to be the center of the maze. There was a huge stone fountain surrounded by bright red rose bushes. Eight paths led into the center, and eight grey stone benches sat between the maze exits. There was evidence Grissall and Xalph had been here—a discarded leather shoe, a blue hair ribbon hanging from a branch, but otherwise, we were alone.

"They're not here." I sat on one of the benches.

"They probably already found their way to dinner," Arun said, taking a seat beside me on the same bench.

I groaned, but secretly, I didn't mind the time with Arun. It was nice to be able to talk to someone who wouldn't brush off my concerns or tell me I was silly for feeling a certain way.

"You know, I never felt like a Phina." Arun spoke casually, as if the words meant nothing to him, but when he glanced over at me, his smile was tight, his eyes wary and guarded.

"What do you mean?" I asked.

"You remember how I told you we're cast out at thirteen? Meant to find our way back home on our own with a bow constructed by our own hand?"

I nodded. When I'd turned thirteen, my father had given me my ax and sent me off to train with Erik and Estrid. It had been one of the best days of my life. I wondered if Arun felt the same, if he'd been just as excited. Or if striking out on his own had been too frightening to really enjoy.

"I stayed away for years," he confessed, "even after I'd made the bow and retrieved the raptor owl feather. I didn't want to go back. I didn't want to live the life of a High Elf that was expected of me. I loved life beyond the walls, below the veil. This was all I wanted." He waved a hand around.

"A hedge maze?" I bumped his shoulder and smiled over at him.

He narrowed his eyes at me. "No. Adventure. Friends. A cause worth fighting for."

"I hope you don't think I'm that cause—"

"No," he said quickly. "I guess what I'm trying to say is … plans change. I was raised to be one thing and found my calling doing something else. And you know what? When I went home finally and confessed to my mother how I felt, do you know what she said?"

"What?"

"She said, 'That's nice, dear. As long as you're happy.' And then proceeded to feed me until it was time for me to leave again."

I laughed. "I think I would like your mother."

"I think you would, too," he said, his voice quieter than it had been. "Give your brother and sister some credit. Be who you're meant to be, and they'll be there for you."

I was suddenly very aware of how close we were sitting. There were seven other benches, but he'd sat beside me, the whole side of his body pressed against mine. There was a part of me that wanted to bolt to my feet and put as much distance between us as possible, but there was another part of me that wanted to lean into him and let myself fall just a little bit.

I cleared my throat and focused on the fountain. It was at least twice my height, and at the top was the likeness of a man I assumed to be Onen Suun. "Will you be going home soon?"

He shifted, leaning slightly away from me. So, the weird tension I'd felt wasn't one-sided. "I'm in no rush," he answered.

"Why not? Don't you want to see your mother?" If I could, I would already be in Bor'sur. I longed for the day when my father would wrap me in his arms again.

He shrugged. "Elves are not particularly maternal. She has her own life, and I have mine. I have no real reason to go back. All I have is a bunch of land and a big, empty house. I show up every now and then to check on things, but the caretakers are plenty competent. They don't need me there to keep things running."

"What about Tsarra?" She was the woman who'd sent me down this path, hiring me to go into the mines to free Arun so he could save her family. Even though she was ultimately to credit for his freedom, he had hardly mentioned her.

"Another one of my causes." One side of his mouth tilted up into a humorless smile. "I don't know. Marrying her would be the end, wouldn't it? I'd be tied down. It would be the only truly selfless thing I'd ever done. I guess I'm just not ready for it."

"I don't know. I think going after that dragon was pretty selfless."

It was the whole reason he'd been on Barepost. Governor

Luthair had imprisoned a dragon after the dragon and some of his friends had destroyed one of Luthair's trading vessels. The dragon's friends had enlisted Arun to go into Barepost and negotiate the dragon's freedom. Arun had succeeded—in a sense —winning the dragon's freedom only at the cost of his own.

This time, his laugh was real, rumbling up from his chest. "I went after that dragon because I would have taken any excuse to get out of Lamruil. Luthair himself could have summoned me and I would have come running."

"To get out of Lamruil or to get away from Tsarra?" The picture he was painting was becoming a bit clearer, but it didn't make me like him any less. If anything, it was good to see that his honor had flaws like everyone else's.

He clapped a hand on my knee, the contact startling. "A little bit of both, I think. They kind of feel like they're one and the same." He stood then, releasing me. "We should probably report for dinner."

I stood, too. "Arun—" I started, reaching out and touching the back of his arm. He turned, eyes searching my face. I didn't know what I wanted to say, only that I didn't want this, whatever this was, to end. Not yet. We stood frozen, my hand on his arm, my mouth open to speak words I hadn't figured out yet.

And that was when the screaming started.

# CHAPTER 4

The screams were coming from the direction of the temple, but I couldn't see anything except for the tops of leafy green hedges. Then, movement in the sky drew my eye.

"No." The word came out as a breath, a quiet exhalation of fear.

Large, human-shaped bodies were silhouetted against the sinking sun, wings sprouting from broad backs.

The ur'gels had found us.

Had found *me*, if Beru was right and they were looking for the Suun heir. Or who they thought was the Suun heir.

Another scream shook Arun and me from our stupor.

"Go," Arun said, but he didn't have to tell me. I was already running, kicking up dirt and leaves as I threw myself down the nearest path.

And ran headlong into a dead end. "Damn it."

"This way." Arun grabbed my hand and tugged me back, taking a turn to the left I had bypassed.

Increased shouts were rising from the temple, and all I could imagine were the girls in their orange robes being scooped up like rabbits by a raptor owl. I hoped Xalph and Grissall, wherever they were, had taken cover.

Arun and I ran through what felt like endless twists and turns, the temple growing gradually closer. We reached another dead end and were turning around when Arun stopped, grabbing me by my shoulders and turning me to face whatever it was he saw. An ur'gel was almost directly overhead, and in his arms he carried … a body. Human or elf, I couldn't be sure, but it draped from its arms, limbs twitching.

Were the ur'gels taking prisoners? Hostages? Trophies? Had this body come from the temple or was it someone from the nearby town Lunla had mentioned? Had the ur'gels already wreaked their havoc there?

To my horror, the ur'gel dropped its cargo. The body crashed into the hedge not far from us, crushing leaves and branches before rolling to the ground, facedown.

"Onen save us," Arun said, more to himself than to me.

The body was slender and draped in a black robe. Long, black hair fell across her back.

"Is she …?"

"I don't know."

She wasn't moving. I crept forward and nudged her with the toe of my boot. No response. I knelt and rolled her over.

The woman—the corpse?—lunged at me, fingers outstretched and teeth snapping. I caught her at arm's length, my hands going around her neck and pressing her to the ground.

Her face was more a skull than an actual face. A thin layer of skin stretched over sharp bones. Lips peeled back to reveal two rows of yellow teeth. Worst of all, though, were her eyes. Gaping black holes stared back at me. She'd been a human woman once, but she was something else now, somewhere between dead and alive.

I was stunned, frozen with my hands around her neck. Her

hands reached for me, claw-like fingernails scraping the skin of my arms. It was Arun who lifted me off her. Without my weight holding her down, she crawled forward, her movements jerky and unnatural as she grasped for Arun's legs. She made a low hissing noise and he scrambled back, knocking into me, sending us both sprawling.

The corpse wrapped a hand around my ankle and I kicked, my boot connecting with her jaw. It should have knocked her off, but she didn't even react. Instead, she continued her slow, steady progress up my leg.

My fingers fumbled for my ax, clumsy and trembling. I'd faced warriors twice my size, monsters with more teeth and stingers than I could count. But I had always known what I was facing, and I had always known how to win.

Arun was there then, standing over her and lifting her off by her shoulders. He didn't have any weapons, just his bare hands. She twisted, driving him back with her snapping jaw. I stood, finally drawing my ax, and swung. The blade sliced through the skull easier than it should have. Finally, the body fell to the ground leaving a stunned, blood-splattered Arun looking at me.

"What was that?" He wiped at his face with his sleeve, staining the white fabric red.

"I don't—I—" I thought I was going to be sick. Blood pooled at my feet, matting in her black hair. Her mouth and eyes still gaped open. The world narrowed to just me and her, the edges of my vision going black.

"I didn't know how—she wouldn't stop—"

Arun took my shoulders in his hands and shook them gently. I looked up at him and the roiling in my gut calmed at the sight of his dark brown eyes.

"We have to go," he said. "If this is what they're facing at the temple, they need us."

With that, the rest of the world came rushing back. The smell of the dead girl, the screams from the temple, the howling and grunting of the ur'gels as they flew overhead. It was chaos. I was supposed to be good in chaos. I *was* good in chaos. I just had to remember that.

I led the way this time, and Arun followed without comment. Keeping my wits about me made it easier to find our way out.

When we emerged into the yard, it was worse than I'd imagined. Erik and Estrid were fighting back-to-back, surrounded by dozens of walking corpses in black cloaks, all of them with those same gaping eye sockets. I watched as one of them fell on a girl in orange robes who had been foolishly fleeing across the grounds. Before I could move to help her, Stiarna was there, ripping the corpse away from the girl and separating its head from its body with her powerful beak. The corpse grew still and Stiarna dove back into the fray.

There was a shout from behind us in the maze. We turned at the same time and watched an ur'gel rise from the hedges with a girl in its clutches. This wasn't a placid corpse, though. This girl was fighting for all she was worth, kicking and hitting the ur'gel who was struggling to get very far off the ground.

"It's Grissall," I said. They hadn't made it out of the maze after all.

The ur'gel rose a few feet in the air and that was when I understood why it was struggling. Attached to Grissall's legs was Xalph, his arms wrapped tight around her ankles. Both of them were screaming, but there was no way I would make it there in time.

But I didn't have to. Arun raised the bow he wore strapped across his back and nocked an arrow. Together, we watched the ur'gel gain more height, but it wasn't a smooth flight. It dipped and wove as it fought against Grissall and Xalph.

"Hurry," I urged him, "before it gets too high."

"I can't get a clean shot," Arun murmured. He held the string of the bow tight, drawn against the corner of his mouth.

"Just take it."

He did, releasing the arrow just as the ur'gel opened its leathery wings wide to catch a current. The arrow hit the monster in the throat. It dropped Grissall. She and Xalph plummeted into the hedges, but the ur'gel still struggled to stay aloft. Arun nocked another arrow and let it fly, hitting it in the chest and sending it spiraling down into the bushes.

"Go help them." I put a hand on his shoulder and pushed him back toward the maze. "I'm going to help my brother and sister."

Arun didn't argue. He kept his bow ready as he disappeared around the first corner, shouting for Xalph.

I dove into the battle in the yard, my ax in one hand and my sword in the other. My left shoulder was sore, but it wasn't unbearable. I hoped Erik was hanging in there in spite of the pain in his burned arm.

The fighters were mostly the walking corpses. It seemed the ur'gels had simply dropped their weapons and fled, probably hoping to come back later and reap the rewards once the dirty work was done. I fell into a rhythm—a sideways swing of my ax across one's temple, a downward slice of my sword to behead the one behind it. I cut my way through the attackers until I reached Erik and Estrid.

"Frida!" Estrid yelled as she drove both of her swords up into the chins of two walking corpses. "Where have you been?"

"Doesn't matter." I reached past her and pushed the blade of my sword into the forehead of a corpse-man who had been coming up just behind her. It fell, knocking back another one beside it. "I'm here now."

Erik grunted as he dispatched two more corpses. "Where's your elf?"

"He's getting Grissall and Xalph in the maze." There was a corpse on the ground. I planted my foot on its chest. Its fingers clawed at my boot but when I put my sword through its head, it grew still.

"What do you mean, 'your elf'?" Estrid asked, turning her head to look at Erik even as she fought off one of the attackers.

Erik laughed. "Do you mean you haven't noticed?" He spun, knocking aside three corpses at once.

"What are you talking about?" I jerked my sword out of a corpse's eye and turned, driving it through another one's chest. It stumbled back but didn't fall. Instead, it ripped the sword out of my grip and looked up at me. It opened its mouth and hissed, lunging forward.

An arrow through its temple sent it toppling sideways.

I looked up to see Arun standing on a bench, felling one corpse after another with arrows. Xalph and Grissall were beside him, knives at the ready in case any got too close. When he saw me looking, he raised his chin in acknowledgement and winked.

"*That's* what I'm talking about," Erik answered.

I ignored him. Mainly because I didn't know how to respond.

Estrid was watching me, though, possibly waiting for a denial.

"Watch out," I told her.

She ducked, and I drove the butt of my ax into the face of a corpse behind her. It crushed the nose in and cracked the eye sockets, but it kept coming. Estrid swung her sword, slicing clean through the neck. The body hit the ground, head rolling away.

Across the courtyard, there was another shout, this one loud enough to be heard over the din. I shoved my way out of the crush of bodies surrounding me and my siblings and saw Lunla on the temple steps, struggling with a corpse. She had her hands around its throat, but it was snapping and clawing at her. She was barely hanging on.

Arun and I began running for her at the same time, but I was surrounded by fallen bodies. I was clambering over them, tripping over splayed limbs and trying not to step on any faces. Arun reached the priest first, but he didn't have a weapon viable for close combat, only his bow. He swung it at the corpse's head. It turned and Lunla shoved it away, hitting Arun. He tripped down the last step and fell, the creature on top of him. I was nearly there when it sunk its teeth into his shoulder. Arun screamed, and I swung my ax at its head, the force of the blow knocking the corpse to the side. I brought my sword down with my other hand into its neck, and finally, it stopped moving.

It was only then, as the head rolled to a stop, the crushed face pointed to the sky, that I realized it had grown quiet. Stiarna jumped up onto a retaining wall nearby and began to lick her front feet, her face and beak covered in blood. Erik and Estrid rushed over, Xalph and Grissall close behind them.

I dropped to my knees beside Arun. "Are you okay?"

He grunted. His face twisted with pain.

I tore the shirt away from his shoulder and examined the wound. The teeth had broken the skin, and the wound was already red and inflamed.

"Here." Lunla appeared beside me. Her hands shook as she put them on Arun's arm. "Let me."

I moved aside to let her look.

"What was that?" Xalph asked.

No one answered, because no one knew. We were surrounded by destroyed, mutilated bodies. Bodies that, though they hadn't been alive, had been trying to kill us. Bodies that had been carried here and dropped on us by ur'gels, servants of Dag'draath, if legends were to be believed. Their blood soaked into the grass and spread across the stone paths.

Girls in orange robes walked among them, quiet with shock. I watched one kneel at the head of one of the bodies. After a few seconds, she fell back and scrambled away.

"This one's alive!"

I didn't have the energy left to hurry over, so I left it to Erik.

He stepped over the circle of bodies at the base of the temple steps and stood over the one the girl had indicated. He studied the body for longer than I thought necessary, and then, to all our surprise, knelt and took its hand in his.

"What is it?" Estrid called to him.

He stood and turned back to us. "It's Savarah," he said, his eyebrows knit together in confusion. "She's alive."

# CHAPTER 5

I left Arun's side and crossed the yard to where Erik was. The girl on the ground wore the same black cloak as the corpses. Her hood was thrown back, revealing a halo of golden curls. Her eyes were closed, but I recognized her round cheeks and full lips.

Savarah was the companion to Tsarra Trisfina, the elf who had hired me to get Arun Phina out of the mines. We'd lost her back on the climb to the plateau and assumed she'd fallen and died. Had she been taken instead? Had her body been stolen by the ur'gels and turned into one of their weapons.

But Erik, and the girl, had said she was alive. I knelt, putting a hand on Savarah's wrist. The pulse there was strong.

"Savarah?" I said, gently shaking her.

The girl's eyes snapped open.

I gasped, jerking back.

"Frida?" Her voice was hoarse and low, her eyes wide with surprise.

"Savarah, what are you doing here?" I asked.

Erik didn't wait for an answer. He all but pushed me aside to get to her, putting his arm beneath her shoulders and lifting her to her feet. She looked around, taking in the sight of the bodies and the temple that towered over them.

"Where am I?" she asked.

"One of the temples of light, still on Bruhier." Erik kept his arms around her, holding her up as she surveyed her surroundings.

I didn't like this. It felt wrong. *She* felt wrong. I was about to tell Erik as much when there was a hand on my shoulder. I turned to see Lunla there, her usually stoic face twisted with worry.

"Your elf is not well," she said.

What was with everyone calling him 'my elf'? "What do you mean? It was just a bite." All of us had suffered worse. Perhaps this priest, isolated as she was, had never seen battle wounds.

She shook her head. "It appears that the bite infected him with some type of poison, perhaps."

"Not poison," Savarah interjected. We turned to her, where she still stood beside Erik. "Did you say that one of your people was bitten by a cadaver?"

"Yes, Arun Phina."

Strangely, the name brought no specific recognition to her face. She just nodded solemnly. "Not poison," she repeated. "Infection. He's been infected. I'm sorry to say that he will soon become a living cadaver."

I whipped around to Lunla, Savarah forgotten. "Can't you do something?"

Lunla, typically calm and composed, actually grimaced. "I've never seen anything like this. This is no infection I know how to treat."

I looked over her shoulder. Arun had grown deathly still where he'd fallen on the steps. "Can't you, I don't know … use the light?" I waved my hands around, encompassing the temple and the grounds around it.

The priest visibly steeled herself, straightening her shoulders and wiping the fear from her face, before summoning several of her girls. The golden-haired priests-in-training were not so eager to help as they had been before. They approached slowly, as if expecting Arun to turn on them.

"Take him to the infirmary," Lunla ordered.

"I'm coming with you." I moved toward the girls to help lift him but drew up short when one waved her hand and Arun rose effortlessly into the air and floated up the steps.

"She's an air elemental," Lunla explained.

As a D'ahvol, I had no magic, even with my elven ancestry. It was easy to forget, sometimes, how much of it truly existed in the world.

When Arun disappeared inside with the priests, I turned to the others, all of whom were checking each other over for bite marks. Only Savarah stood still and uninterested.

I took two large steps toward her and jabbed a finger into her chest. "It's time for you to tell us how you know that about the infection, and how you got here."

It was Erik who pushed me away from her. "You don't have to answer anything until you're ready."

I rolled my eyes so hard I worried they might get stuck in the back of my head.

"I don't mind." Savarah looked up at him through her ridiculously long lashes. "But maybe something to eat while we talk?"

Erik ushered her inside the temple and the rest of us followed, Estrid and me next, with Grissall and Xalph bringing up the rear. The two had been quiet with everything that happened after the attack, but both of them still clutched their knives.

I dropped back and put an arm around Grissall. "Are you okay?"

She wasn't much younger than I but was considerably smaller. She looked up at me. "I kept thinking I would see Papa among the dead."

Her father had been one of the only people to show me and my siblings any kindness when we'd crash-landed a few years ago. After the ur'gels had attacked Barepost, Gerves had sent her away with us, supposedly so we could keep her safe and she could escape the dangers of Barepost. I didn't think Gerves would be pleased with what had just happened here.

"I wouldn't worry about him," I said, squeezing her narrow shoulders. "Your father can take care of himself." In spite of my empty reassurances, I knew how she felt. I'd left my own father behind in Bor'sur years ago. I held my breath any time news came from the Western March. It was easy, once I got into the habit, to always expect the worst.

We gathered around the dining table, which was still set from the forgotten dinner. The sliced roast pork was frigid, so I grabbed a plateful of fresh vegetables instead, crunching down on a carrot while I watched Savarah take a seat.

I didn't like her and never had. I'd tolerated her because I'd needed something from her, but now the only thing she had I needed was knowledge. And there were ways to get that out of someone which had nothing to do with being nice. There was no way Erik would let me touch her, though. He was filling her plate for her as she pointed to her selections. It was disgusting.

"So," I said when everyone sat down, "let's start at the beginning. What happened to you at the cliff?"

We'd left Barepost to help Arun and the miners escape and had run into some sort of tree monster climbing the cliff face. After fighting it off and taking refuge on a ledge, Savarah had just … disappeared. We'd thought her dead, but had apparently been wrong.

"I was taken." She looked down at her plate. "Snatched by a flying cliff monster while you all had your backs turned. It all happened so fast I couldn't even scream." She pressed a napkin to her mouth.

Erik reached over and patted her back. "You don't have to—"

"No, it's okay." She lowered the napkin and looked up at me. "It took me to its nest and left me for dead, but I was able to escape that night. I was heading back to Barepost when I came across an ur'gel."

"How did you know what it was?" I asked.

She smiled wryly. "I am not so foolish as to believe that legends are not based in fact. Surely, you've seen enough monsters on Bruhier to know better."

I nodded, conceding the point.

"It came after me. I'm good with my knives but I'm not equipped to take on a monster alone. So, I played dead. I thought it would lose interest and leave me alone but instead, it carried me away to one of their camps in the jungle. It was below the veil, but I guess when you're a monster, you don't fear other monsters."

"What did they do to you?" My plate lay forgotten in front of me. I leaned forward, my elbows on the table. I didn't like her, but anyone who had faced the ur'gels deserved at least some respect.

"They were reviving the cadavers, creating their army of the dead with some sort of unfamiliar magic ritual. But I wasn't dead, so the ritual didn't work on me."

"How did you survive?"

"By pretending to be one of them."

The experience she described next had us all riveted in our seats. She'd seen others turned by the ritual, so she'd given the best performance of her life, pretending to change into one of them. The walking corpses were kept in pens like animals, and she'd imitated them to avoid detection. The ur'gels had abused the corpses, beating them just to prove a point—that the creatures could feel no pain or anger. They did only what they were told, with no memory of who they were before the transformation. She'd been living in constant fear of discovery. But according to Savarah, she'd been able to stay out of the way, to hide behind others and create distractions. And the ur'gels were careless, because they assumed they were only dealing with the living dead.

"I had no idea why they were keeping us there, but when I saw the corpses being taken away, I knew I had another decision to make. I could keep playing dead and possibly escape, or I could make a run for it at the camp and risk recapture and true death."

Erik covered one of her hands with his. "You made the right decision."

Savarah nodded, eyes wide and glistening with unshed tears. "I'm so grateful to be back with you all, so grateful to be alive."

After the interrogation that passed for a dinner, we helped the priests clear the yard of the bodies. They were burned in a pyre on the edge of the cliff.

"To avoid the spread of infection," Lunla said. According to her, Arun was still alive, his condition had not improved, and he had not woken again.

That night, I lay in one of the temple's many sparse bedrooms, unable to sleep. Somewhere far below, Arun was fighting for his life. And in another of these rooms, Savarah slept soundly, unconcerned about him or the original quest.

Several restless hours passed before I finally rose from bed and ventured into the dark residential hall. Most of the doors were closed, but at the end of the hall, where there was a sitting room, a fire still burned, the room glowing orange. I tiptoed down the hall and peeked inside.

Erik and Estrid were already there. Estrid sprawled in a high-backed chair, her hair loose. Erik stood before the fire in just his undershirt and loose trousers. It was strange to see them both without their leather armor or weapons.

Estrid looked at me over her shoulder. "Took you long enough."

"You could have come for me." I moved inside the room and

took the chair across from Estrid. "Are you here because of Savarah?"

"Yes," Estrid said at the same time Erik said, "No."

"Then why are you here?" I asked Erik.

He turned away from the fire to survey Estrid and me. "To defend her against you two."

Estrid scoffed and waved a hand dismissively in the air. "I don't want to hear it."

"Come on," I said. "You can't possibly be sympathetic to her. Did you notice she hasn't once mentioned getting back to Tsarra? Tsarra left her in Barepost as a 'trusted advisor.' Shouldn't that be her first objective?"

"You heard for yourself what she's been through."

"I heard what she said," I agreed, "but how do we know that any of it is even true?"

Erik slapped a hand against the wall beside the hearth. "What reason does she have to lie? Why didn't you just ask her about Arun and Tsarra?"

I ran a hand through my short hair and sighed. "Because I didn't want to give her the chance to lie her way out of it." What I didn't add was I wanted to catch her in whatever lie she was telling. I didn't trust her, and I would find a way to prove it to Erik.

But he didn't even entertain the idea. "When he recovers, I'm going to ask Arun to take her to wherever she needs to go."

Over my dead body. "He's not taking her anywhere. She is no one's responsibility."

"You don't think she'll be good to have along?" Estrid chimed in. "She's obviously very resourceful."

My mouth dropped open. What could they possibly be thinking? My only instinct when it came to Savarah was to get as far away as possible. "Let her use her resources to get herself home, then. We don't owe her anything."

Estrid and Erik exchanged a glance that made my blood boil.

I rose from the chair and stormed out, leaving them to talk about me in peace.

# CHAPTER 6

Even in the dark hallways, I found my way to the temple where I knew there would be a priest at the altar. It seemed that someone was stationed there all day and night, tending the fire and wiping up any water spilled by worshipers. I wasn't disappointed. A young girl was stoking the fire with an iron rod.

She turned when I approached and lowered her head in a small bow of acknowledgment.

I nodded back at her. "Do you know where I can find the infirmary?" I asked.

The priest gave me directions and a stone I recognized as yooperlite. Arun and I had found a whole cave of it back in the mine on Barepost. As I held the rock in my hand, warming it, it began to glow, acting as a small light to guide me through the dark halls.

Following her directions, I returned to the residential tower and descended into the lower levels until I reached a heavy wooden door with an iron ring. I used the ring to knock twice, and the door groaned open. Another priest, barely distinguishable from the girl in the temple, blinked at me.

I held the yooperlite high. "I'd like to see Arun Phina," I said. When she didn't seem to understand, I added, "The elf."

"Of course." She beckoned me inside and I followed her down a cool stone hallway.

"It's so cold down here," I commented, rubbing my arms as we walked. I was still in my nightshirt, the cool air raising the hairs on my arms.

She looked over her shoulder at me. "We find that heat breeds infection. That's why the infirmary is down here, where the sun cannot reach and warm the sickrooms."

I followed her into one of the rooms on the right. It was sparsely furnished with just a small bed, a wooden chair beside it, and a dresser with a warped mirror and wash basin. Arun was on the bed, the light sheet pulled down and tucked around his waist. His top half was naked, except for a blood-soaked bandage on his left shoulder.

There were dark stones placed in strange patterns on the hard planes of his chest and stomach. Lunla stood over him, her head bowed and her hands hovering over the stones. There was a strange vibration in the room that made me stop in the doorway. D'ahvol weren't just without magic, we were immune to it. Even still, I could feel it flowing around Lunla and Arun. A strange external force filling the room.

It stopped abruptly when Lunla looked up and saw us standing there. Her hands fell to her sides. Arun grunted, but didn't move or open his eyes.

"How is he?" I asked, still in the doorway.

"He's healing." She looked down at him. "I think."

"I couldn't sleep, so I just wanted to check on him." I gestured to the chair. "I can sit with him if you need a break."

Lunla smiled at that, as if it were a ridiculous idea. "There's no need for that, but I am glad you're here. There's something we should talk about."

My stomach dropped. I didn't really feel much like talking,

especially if it was going to go anything like my talk with Erik and Estrid. But I couldn't very well say no, so when she beckoned me forward I followed, taking a seat in the chair by the bed. It was close enough to Arun I could reach up and take his hand where it lay on the edge of the bed without drawing any attention to the contact.

Lunla and the other priest didn't seem to notice. They were busy taking the stones off Arun and dropping them into a black bag. When they were done, Lunla cinched the bag closed and passed it to the girl, who took it with obvious reluctance.

"Take these to the temple fire. We will burn the sickness out of him."

The girl spun on a heel and left, practically running down the hall.

Then, Lunla turned to me. "Because of what you and your friends did for us—for me—I want to offer you guidance on your journey."

"That would be helpful," I said carefully, not sure where this was going. Not sure I wanted her guidance.

She perched herself on the edge of Arun's bed. The elf didn't stir. "If you want to find out more about the Suun heir, then you need to find the Sisters of Light."

The Sisters of Light? It sounded familiar. I remembered Beru telling Lunla their search for the Light Woman had been a dead end. I wondered if they were related, and if this would also lead nowhere. But I didn't say anything, because it wasn't like I had any other idea what to do or where to go. As much as I wanted to go home, I couldn't lead all this trouble back to Bor'sur and my father. Proving I wasn't the Suun heir was the only way I would be able to get clear of this mess and go home again.

"Where can I find these sisters?" I asked.

"Last I heard, they reside above the Valley of the Horses."

"Horses? On Bruhier?" Surely, she was mistaken. It was practically impossible to keep horses on Bruhier. Loyal though they were, they had almost zero survival instinct and were perfect monster fodder. And they certainly weren't equipped to climb the cliffs to safety.

"Yes." She smiled a secretive smile. "There are some things on this island you just have to see for yourself."

I thought I'd seen quite enough already, but I guessed I would have to endure still more before this journey was over.

From the bed, Arun stirred.

I dropped his hand and wiped my palms on the bottom of my tunic, embarrassed I had forgotten I was even holding it.

His eyes opened slowly, blinked once, and then he turned to me. He gave me a small, weak smile. "Am I dead?"

"No." I couldn't help but smile back.

Lunla stood and stared at him. "It worked," she said, more to herself than to either of us.

Arun coughed and grimaced, as if it hurt. "Are you sure? I feel dead."

"I assure you, you're not." Lunla was circling him. She pulled down his lower eyelid and peered inside his eyes, then checked his pulse with two fingers on his neck, her eyes closed as she counted the beats. Then, to me, "Stay with him. I need to go to the temple."

I nodded, and she left at a trot, faster than I'd seen her move yet.

When she'd left, Arun shifted in the bed so that he was angled toward me. "What happened?"

"You were bitten."

"Bitten? By ... a corpse?"

"While saving Lunla's life," I confirmed. "Apparently, the bite could have turned you into one of them, but Lunla was able to stop the spread of infection."

"How?"

I shrugged. "Magic?"

He chuckled quietly but held a hand to his chest as if even that small movement hurt him. "You don't sound so sure about that."

"I guess...," I paused. It wasn't every day I opened up to people, but I reminded myself this was Arun. He was easy to talk to and never judged. "I guess it's hard to believe in magic when it has no effect on me or my people. It's easy to label it some ridiculous idea until I see it performed before my eyes."

"Like flying ships?"

"Like a man brought back from the edge of death."

He was quiet for a beat. "It was that bad?"

"It was that bad."

Silence fell between us and Arun closed his eyes, his face gradually relaxing. As I watched him, I thought about what Lunla had said and wondered how long it would be before he was recovered enough to take us to find the Valley of the Horses. If we couldn't fly there, it meant walking. Bruhier was not a small place. Walking aimlessly through the valleys with their monsters and other hidden dangers was a fool's errand. Worst of all, Erik and Estrid would never agree to it.

"I cannot sleep with you thinking so loud." Arun spoke without opening his eyes or even turning his face toward me.

"Sorry," I said.

He opened his eyes then. "What are you thinking about?"

Maybe it was selfish to tell him now, when he was still so sick, but I didn't think he would mind having something else to think about for a little while. "Lunla told me to find the Sisters of Light if I wanted to find out more about the heir."

"And I assume you do?" He shifted slightly, obviously uncomfortable.

I reached behind his head and fluffed the feather pillows, situating them so he would be propped up a bit. "I have to," I answered finally. "I can't go home if everyone thinks I'm this Suun heir. It would lead the ur'gels right to the Western March and put even more people in danger." Most importantly my father. He had done so much to protect me and guide me that I couldn't do that to him, no matter how angry I was with him for potentially keeping secrets about my mother from me. Secrets that would one day change my life.

"Who are the Sisters of Light?" Arun asked.

"I was hoping you would know."

He furrowed his brow in thought. "I know we're in a temple of light, and Lunla is a priest who worships the light. So, I assume the Sisters have something to do with the same thing. Maybe it's another temple."

"Maybe." Why wouldn't she have just said that, though?

"Did she say anything else?"

"That they're near the Valley of the Horses."

Arun scoffed, much as I had when I'd first heard the name. "There are no horses on Bruhier. Have you ever heard of it?"

I shook my head. "I was hoping you had."

"No, but I'll help you find it." He pushed himself up on his arms, groaned, and fell back. All the color had drained from his face with that one movement. "Just as soon as I can get up."

"When might that be?"

"Soon," he said.

I raised my eyebrows at him.

"I'm an elf," he said as if that explained everything. "It won't be long. All you have to worry about is getting your family rounded up. I think you might have the harder job of the two."

It was my turn to groan.

Silence fell between us again, and this time Arun did sleep. His breathing grew steady and his face relaxed. Lunla and the healer priest returned shortly after, carrying more smooth black stones. I left him in their capable hands and went to find Erik and Estrid. I didn't know how, but I would find a way to get them on that ship and leave Savarah behind, where she could find her own way home.

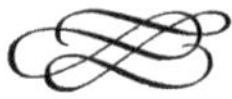

# CHAPTER 7

The sun had risen by the time I made my way out of the infirmary wing, and the temple was bustling with activity.

A pair of girls passed me in the hall carrying a bucket and two mops. "It was your turn to clean the floors," one of them said.

The other girl huffed a sigh. "Don't be stupid. I cleaned them yesterday."

I watched them pass. I'd never heard any of the priests speak more than a few words, and to hear them being mean to each other felt wrong. Outside the dining hall, I found Xalph and Grissall lounging on the stone floor, sharing a sliced orange.

"I wouldn't go in there if I were you," Xalph said around an orange peel he had stuck in front of his teeth.

"Why not?"

He shrugged. "Don't say I didn't warn you."

I entered the room against his better judgment. Erik sat at the head of the table, his knife and fork held in his hands like weapons. To his right, Estrid stood, both of her hands planted flat on the table as she towered over him. On his other side, Savarah sat casually buttering a piece of toast.

"You're an insufferable know-it-all," Estrid was saying to our brother.

Erik, who was at times an insufferable know-it-all, shrugged. "And you're a control freak."

Savarah took a long swig of the orange juice in front of her. Then, "Seems to me that you're both just stating the obvious."

"I can't take it anymore." Estrid slammed her hands down on the table, rattling the glasses and silverware.

"Then you should have just let me stay in Barepost like I told you to."

"Erik!" I said, my voice sharp.

Both of them turned to look at me, anger still twisting their features.

Savarah glanced at me, and then back at her breakfast. "I told them to stop. They wouldn't listen."

I found that hard to believe. The woman seemed to thrive on discord. "What are you even fighting about?"

Neither of them answered. Estrid's mouth flopped open and closed like a fish gasping for breath out of water, but nothing came out. Did they even know why they were calling each other names in the middle of breakfast?

Savarah leaned back in her chair and surveyed the three of us. "They're fighting over me."

It wouldn't be the first time Erik and Estrid had fought over a girl, but did it have to be this girl? "What about you?"

"What to do with me."

This felt familiar.

"She's coming with us," Estrid said, finding her voice again.

"She's going home." Erik snapped his eyes to Savarah. "If you want. We'll take you wherever you need to go."

"No, we won't," I interjected, joining the argument.

Savarah smiled at me, looking amused. "Let me guess. You want to leave me here."

I pulled out the chair beside Estrid and sat down heavily, tired of this same fight. "Our journey is not yours. There's something that I have to do, and my brother and sister are going with me." Channeling Lunla, I added, "Here is where our paths divide."

"Oh, you have a plan now?" Estrid rolled her eyes at Erik. Now that they could gang up on me, they were on the same side again. "Where are we going?"

I glanced up at Savarah and then quickly away when I caught her looking back at me. "I'd rather not say in front of present company."

The door to the kitchens swung open and the sound of raised voices drifted out to us before it swung shut again. A young priest with flushed red cheeks refilled Savarah's juice glass and eyed the table.

"We're fine, thank you," Savarah told her.

We were definitely not fine—it didn't seem like anyone was. Ever since the battle with the walking corpses, everyone in the temple had been on edge, like a line of galestone waiting to ignite. No, not since the battle. Since we'd found Savarah. And she hadn't even tried to defend herself when I'd voiced my mistrust of her.

I stamped down the anger building inside of me and looked up to find Savarah still studying me across the table.

"What is that mark beside your eye?" she asked, tapping a finger to her chin.

I reached up and touched the five-pointed star without even thinking about it. If Beru were to be believed, it was the mark of Onen Suun, designating me as one of his descendants. Not a blessing, but a curse.

"I don't know," I answered finally.

Her eyes narrowed, her otherwise smooth skin wrinkling on her brow. "Well, what do you think it means?"

"What I think doesn't matter. It's just a birthmark." I hoped Erik and Estrid would keep their mouths shut. I didn't want Savarah knowing any more than she already did. Thankfully, they had turned their attentions to eating and were mostly ignoring me.

Before Savarah could continue her interrogation, the door to the dining hall opened. Grissall and Xalph pranced through, talking excitedly. Behind them was Arun, leaning heavily on a man in the orange robes of the temple. It was the first man I'd seen this entire time, but it wasn't surprising. Priests could be male or female, as long as they served the light.

The four of us around the table stood and watched his slow progress across the dining hall. He was wearing a loose shirt that gaped at the neck, revealing the edge of the white bandage over the wound on his shoulder. His hair was loose and stringy, and his eyes were sunken into his face, ringed with black. He very nearly looked like a walking corpse.

Erik cleared his throat and we all jerked to life. "Arun, it's so good to see you doing better."

Savarah pulled out the chair beside her. "Yes, it's incredible." Her voice was quiet, her eyes wide, as if she hadn't believed he could be saved.

Arun sank into the chair, releasing his hold on the priest. The man bowed and took his leave while Grissall and Xalph descended on the table like a pair of hungry dogs. They snatched pastries and fruit, stuffing them in their mouths, while the rest of us watched Arun catch his breath.

I watched Arun grimace and shift in his seat. "I can't believe Lunla let you out of bed."

"It's … incredible," Savarah said again.

Arun reached for the plate of pastries. "It wasn't without her objection."

"When will you be able to sail?" Erik asked.

The door opened again and Lunla entered. "He'll need several more treatments. It will take at least another day, and that's if we hurry." Her face was outwardly serene as she crossed the room, but there was a tightness to her small smile that wasn't normally present. My guess was Arun put it there.

Savarah was twirling one of her golden curls around a finger. "What kind of treatments?" she asked.

Lunla studied her for a long, tense moment, and I thought she wouldn't answer. Finally, she said, "It is only light that chases away the dark. I am using the light of my own soul to heal him, but I do not know if it will be enough. It may be that we need a brighter soul to fight the darkness of the spell that is working its way through him."

That explained what she'd been doing when I'd come to his room earlier, the strange vibrations of magic in the infirmary. It stood to reason a priest would not heal with medicines and herbs, but with light and magic. It was still hard for me to believe, but the proof was sitting right across from me, licking sugar from his fingers.

"Tomorrow, then," Arun said.

Lunla patted his head as if she were humoring a small child. "Or, perhaps, the next day."

Arun looked around the table and gave a small shrug. "There's really no arguing with her."

While Arun spent the day under Lunla's ministrations, I spent it avoiding Savarah and my siblings. I hunted with Stiarna in the woods on the edge of the plateau and brought back a string of pheasants to Cook. The woman was so happy she gave me a whole tray of strawberry cakes Stiarna and I ate while perched on the edge of the cliff, my legs dangling over the abyss.

In the afternoon, I followed one of the younger priests, whose name was Jyne, around the gardens while she pointed out different plants and their uses. I'd met her before, that morning in the infirmary, when I'd gone to visit Arun. She was training to be a healer and working closely with Lunla and Arun. And she was surprisingly good company, easy to talk to, and willing to share.

"What do you think?" I asked when she stopped to pull a red-stemmed weed from the dirt. "Will he be able to leave tomorrow?"

She straightened and shrugged, wiping a bead of sweat from her wide, freckled brow. "This isn't any normal sickness. This won't be cured with a brewed tonic that I can mix up in the pharmacy." She tossed the weed into a nearby trash bin that was being dragged around by another gardener.

We turned and continued our walk. She pointed out a three-leafed plant she said was good for headaches when brewed in hot water. I steered the conversation back to Arun. "He seems to be doing better, though."

She grunted, keeping her eyes on the plants at our feet. "Sure, but at what cost?"

"What do you mean?"

"You know, that's why I wanted to study healing. I don't have any magic, but it's like magic, isn't it? Chasing away sickness with potions, fixing people with my bare hands. But there's one big difference." We'd reached the stone garden wall, and she pulled herself up, perching on top and placing her basket beside her. "Healing is external. Everything comes from outside of me, is separated from me. But magic is internal. What Lunla is doing …" She trailed off, her eyes distant.

"What is Lunla doing?"

"She's using her own life force to heal him. Giving him bits and pieces of herself to put him back together."

I'd never heard anyone speak of magic with such mistrust before, but it was interesting. I'd never been partial to it myself, but I'd thought it was just because I was D'ahvol. To hear a human—a priest, no less—be suspicious of it felt kind of vali-dating. "What does that mean?" I asked.

She pulled a vine from her basket and began plucking the deep green leaves off the stem, dropping them onto her lap. "It means that they will be bound to one another. Depending on how much of herself she gives to him, his life might be bound to hers, or to some talisman she gives him. It's a scary thing, I imagine, to live on someone else's time."

There was so much more I wanted to ask. Did Arun under-stand what was happening and what that meant for him for the rest of his life? Did it have to be Lunla who was bound to him? And most importantly, what would happen if Arun, tired of fighting, gave in to the darkness one day?

But Jyne was done talking. She hopped down from the stone wall and we continued our stroll through the garden. I trailed behind her, listening to her point out different plants and their uses—this one for congestion, that one for infections. None of them, though, seemed to be exactly right for what was ailing me.

# CHAPTER 8

I left Jyne at the door to the infirmary soon afterward and made my way back outside where I had less of a chance of running into my brother or sister. While I was there, Xalph enlisted me to help him map out the hedge maze. I wound my way through it, unspooling a red thread as I went. Xalph and Grissall were behind me, Grissall measuring the paths with her steps while Xalph drew the maze on a piece of wrinkled paper.

"Isn't this cheating?" I called back to them at one point as I backtracked after making a wrong turn.

Xalph's voice carried through the bushes. "It's only cheating if it's against the rules."

I couldn't argue with that.

It didn't take as long this time for me to reach the center of the maze. When I did, I was surprised to see Estrid there, staring at the figure of Onen Suun on top of the enormous fountain, her hands on her hips.

"Why do you look like you want to rip him down?" I asked, only half joking.

She startled, turning to me. "I thought I heard the kid."

"I'm helping him." I motioned to the string wound around my hand as if that explained anything. "What are you doing here?"

"I needed to get away. I haven't felt like myself lately." She began to pace, her nervous energy almost palpable.

"You haven't acted like yourself either."

This made her stop and snap her attention to me.

"Not since we found Savarah," I added. I needed to see if she could be made to see the truth of what was happening.

She was quick to say, "That's ridiculous," and roll her eyes. But in the silence that fell between us, I could see her thinking, analyzing all our recent interactions—the tension between us all when we first heard Savarah's story, the fight in the sitting room, the argument at breakfast. We hadn't had a single peaceful conversation since the girl had turned up, and Estrid was now realizing it.

"It might be ridiculous, but does that make it any less true?" I asked after giving her a few moments to process her thoughts.

She was still trying to reason it away. "If I'm not myself, it's only because you and Erik have been acting too irrationally."

I raised my eyebrows at her. "Really? Just us? You've been perfectly reasonable?"

"Well ..."

Xalph and Grissall emerged from the maze then, a ball of red twine in their hands. "There's one path mapped out," Xalph said, holding the sheet of paper up triumphantly. "Only ..." He spun around in a circle, counting the entrances to the maze. "Eight more to go." Xalph hobbled over to a stone bench, where he sat and began fiddling with his drawing.

Grissall crossed to the fountain and dipped her fingers in the frigid water. "I don't know why you bother," she said. "We'll be leaving soon, surely."

Xalph looked up at me. "Are we leaving?"

"Soon," I told him. "When Arun is able to fly." It occurred to me the two of them might be safer here, at the temple. I would have to talk to Lunla about that later. "You shouldn't give up on your map, though. I'm sure the priests would appreciate having one."

"The priests don't need a map." He rolled his eyes at me as if I were daft. "They use the light to guide them." Xalph stood and was unrolling the string again, handing one end to Grissall.

Grissall tied her end to the stone fountain and disappeared through an entrance, trailing the string after her, Xalph right behind her.

Estrid sat on the recently vacated stone bench and leaned her elbows on her knees. The long side of her hair draped forward, hiding her face from me. "You never did tell us where we were going."

"And I won't, not until I'm sure you won't tell Savarah, or try to bring her along."

Estrid sighed, pushing her hair behind her ear. "I've been thinking about what you said, and I think you're right." Before I could gasp with fake astonishment, she held up a hand. "I don't want to hear it. If I have to, then I'll take it back."

I laughed and sat down beside her, bumping her shoulder with mine.

"What do you think it is?" Estrid asked. "Magic?"

"Can't be. It wouldn't work on us." Then I remembered what Jyne had said about magic being internal. "It must be something external. Something about the way she talks and manipulates us with her words."

"Maybe." Estrid tilted her head back. "What do we even really know about her anyway? Do you believe anything she's told us?"

I shrugged. "It's hard to say. She's supposedly the trusted companion of a High Elf, even though she herself isn't an elf. And she hasn't even mentioned returning Arun to Tsarra.

Wouldn't that be her top priority if she was who she's claimed to be?"

"And what was with her asking about your mark?" Estrid reached over and pushed the hair off my face so she could study the star there.

"She is very curious indeed." I turned away from my sister's probing gaze. She didn't mean anything by it, but I was tired of having everyone look at me differently, even my own siblings. I was still the same Frida as I was before they all thought I was a descendant of Onen Suun.

"Do you trust me now?" Estrid asked. "Will you tell me where we're going?"

I considered her. "Only if you help me get everyone onto the ship without Savarah knowing."

She stuck out her hand. "Fine. Deal."

We shook on it.

"We're going to the Valley of the Horses to seek the Sisters of Light."

Estrid scrunched up her nose in disbelief. "There are no horses on Bruhier."

"That's what I said. But Lunla was certain, and I trust her. After what Arun did for her, I don't think she would lead us wrong."

"Not intentionally, maybe," Estrid added. Then she sat up and clapped her hands together. "So, any ideas how to get everyone out of here and keep Savarah in the dark?"

The red string tied to the fountain twitched, drawing my eye. Xalph and Grissall were on their way back, and I really didn't have time to admire more of Xalph's map or help discover the other paths.

I stood. "I think I know someone who can help."

We exited the maze the way we'd come in. I found myself smiling as we wound through the hedgerows, feeling for the first time in a long time like I finally had someone on my side.

# CHAPTER 9

Arun was alone in the infirmary, sleeping soundly. Estrid and I returned to the kitchen and Cook directed us to an outbuilding where she said they kept the medicinal stores. It was a small, wooden building in the back of the gardens near the tree line. Light shone between the slats. We opened the door and found Jyne hunched over a shelf, shifting around glass jars and muttering to herself.

She straightened and turned to us, blinking in surprise. "Oh," she said. "Hello."

Estrid and I slipped inside and shut the door behind us. Jyne raised the yooperlite stone she held in her hand.

I squinted in the light. I noticed then she was standing in front of a small table. On it was the small leather pouch she usually wore around her waist, and several small jars of green and brown leaves. She was in here restocking. "I hate to ask you for anything, but we need your help," I told her.

"Is this to do with Arun?" she asked.

"Not really."

Estrid was studying a wall of jars to our left, hardly paying attention.

I moved closer to Jyne and lowered my voice. "We need something that will make someone sleep."

She glanced over my shoulder at Estrid. "Is someone not sleeping well?" There was genuine concern on her face.

"No, it's not that." I debated lying to her, but knew it was too risky. We needed someone who knew about these things and would be able to tell us exactly how to do what we needed to do. "It's just that … well, have you met Savarah?"

Jyne visibly shivered at the mention of the name, so I knew she had even before she answered. "Yes, the girl who came in with the corpses."

"Well, we're leaving tomorrow, and she can't come with us."

Understanding dawned on Jyne's face. "Can't you just tell her she can't go? We'll have someone take her to town, so she can find her own way off the plateau."

Estrid had moved to another shelf and was running her finger along faded labels. "It's not that easy," she answered for me. "We can't seem to think straight when she's around. Erik is likely to punch one of us if we try to keep her from getting on the airship."

The yooperlite was fading, so Jyne rubbed it between her hands. It flared back to life as she said, "So, you want her to sleep through your departure, then?"

"Yes, exactly."

She turned her attention to one of the top shelves. The jars there were dusty, the labels barely visible. "I think what you'll want …" She trailed off, standing on tiptoe and moving jars around.

Estrid, who could reach the top shelf with no issue, came up beside her. "Just point."

"Is there one that says vila powder?"

Estrid shifted a few jars aside and then plucked one from the bunch, handing it to Jyne.

After dusting it off, Jyne unscrewed the metal lid and lifted it off. Inside was a light brown powder like sand. "Vila powder is a very potent sleep aid. Just a pinch will knock her out for about an hour."

I took the jar from her and sniffed. There was no obvious smell, which I thought was a good thing. "What would be the dosage for longer than that?"

She was already measuring out small spoonsful into a paper pouch. "I'll give you the proper dosage."

"The proper dosage of what?" came a voice from behind us.

We all whirled toward the door. Lunla stood there, still half in shadow. She stepped inside and coolly surveyed the room. For a moment, none of us spoke.

To my surprise, it was Jyne who stepped forward, sealing the paper bag. "Vila powder. For the elf, in case he needs it on their journey to the valley."

My mouth had been open, ready to defend myself, but I snapped it closed. The priest was lying for us, but it was a flimsy lie. We would, of course, need Arun awake to captain the ship. I glanced at Estrid and then quickly away. I didn't want to give Lunla any reason to be suspicious.

"Hmm." Lunla stepped forward and held her hand out. Jyne dropped the bag of vila powder into the older woman's hand. Lunla pulled it open, glanced inside, and then weighed it in her hand. "For someone Arun's size, you'll need at least another gram." She topped off the bag, sealed it, and handed it to me.

As I tucked it away inside my vest, a warning glance from Jyne told me not to give the full dosage to Savarah. I nodded and turned to Lunla. "May I have a word?" It was true I wanted to talk to her, but this served the second purpose of also distracting her from what we were doing in the shed.

She motioned for me to follow her, and we stepped outside into the night, leaving the others behind. A yooperlite stone in her hand illuminated us in a dull yellow circle. Beyond the gardens, the temple was dark except for candles burning in the windows of the residential hall. We walked slowly down the path.

"What is it, Frida?"

I cleared my throat. "We'll be leaving tomorrow to continue our quest, but I have one more favor to ask you."

She dipped her head at me, her face blank and giving nothing away.

"Could Xalph and Grissall stay here, at the temple?"

"Do you fear they are ill-equipped to deal with the journey?" she asked.

"Actually, no. It's more that I am ill-equipped to keep them safe, and I promised both of their fathers that I would. To do that, I think this is the best place for them, at least for now."

We walked slowly, Lunla's eyes straight ahead. As we neared the temple, she stopped, putting a hand on my arm. "We will allow them to stay on one condition. You must not come back for them."

"What? Why?"

"They have their own destinies, their own parts to play in this conflict, just as you do. Neither of them belongs in Barepost. If they return there, it will be of their own will, and because they are meant to do so."

I didn't know if I could agree to that, to more of Lunla's vague prophesying. But what choice did I have? Drag them along with me and risk their lives, when that was the very thing their fathers had wanted to get them away from? I tried to think of my own father and what he would have wanted for me, but it was not the same. The D'ahvol culture encouraged us to become warriors, to throw ourselves into battle at a young age, to die with honor at the end of an enemy's blade. It wasn't the same for children of miners and innkeepers from Bruhier.

I smiled wryly at Lunla, not even sure if she could see it in the dark. "Fine. Who am I to argue with the word of the light?"

Dinner was served in the dining hall, and all of us, except for

Arun, gathered around the large table to eat. For the first time ever, I made sure to sit beside Savarah. The envelope of vila powder was burning a hole in my vest. I felt like everyone could see it, though of course that was silly. It was just my nerves trying to get the better of me.

Estrid sat on Savarah's other side, beating Erik to the seat by only a few steps. Our brother begrudgingly took the seat on Estrid's left. Between the two of them, surely, they could keep Savarah's attention long enough for me to slip the contents of the envelope into her drink.

We were served fresh brown bread still steaming from the oven, and plates of cabbage and beans. When a man came around and tipped ale into our wooden cups, Estrid put a hand on Savarah's arm. Erik watched her with barely concealed fury as Savarah turned her big, blue eyes on Estrid. Estrid said something I couldn't hear, and Savarah tipped her head back and laughed.

I dug in my vest, my fingers fumbling for the vila powder. Grissall and Xalph were in front of me, but neither of them even glanced in my direction as I drew out the envelope and pulled apart the seal.

"You grew up in Barepost?" I heard Estrid say.

Reaching over, I nudged Savarah's glass closer to me. At the head of the table, Lunla was talking to Grissall, who, Onen bless her, was asking the priest questions about life at the temple. I dumped some of the powder into the cup and then looked into the envelope. There was a little bit left. Jyne had said not to use it all, but what could it hurt to have that extra security? Shrugging to myself, I emptied the packet into the drink just as Savarah reached for it, turning away from my sister.

"And you, Frida?" she asked, lifting the cup to her lips.

"What's that?"

She took a long swig of the drink before answering. "Where will you go when all this is over?"

I watched her for any sign there was something off about the drink, but there was none. "Home. Bor'sur, in the Western March."

"To stay?"

"To see my father. And then, who knows?" I looked across her at Estrid and Erik. "Maybe the three of us will find some other adventure."

Savarah downed her drink and called for another. Not long after, her eyes were drifting shut as they brought out the pastries. She excused herself, looking confused as she explained that she very suddenly wasn't feeling like herself.

Lunla put down her own cup and studied Savarah, who was pushing herself to stand on unsteady feet. "Do you need to go to the infirmary?"

Savarah shook her head. "I just need sleep, I think. I haven't been..." She trailed off and put a hand to her forehead, closing her eyes. "I haven't been sleeping very well." One of the priests took her by her elbow and guided her out of the room.

I made a face at Estrid, who widened her eyes at me, a small smile tugging at the corners of her lips. Over her shoulder, I caught Erik watching me with narrowed eyes. There would be some explaining to do later, but not until I got him away from Savarah.

After dinner, I went outside to search for Stiarna. She'd made herself scarce since the fight, but I found her perched on the bowsprit of the *Iron Duchess*, grooming herself in the blue light of Gleet.

I climbed the hull nets as I'd done the day before, pulling myself up to sit beside her. "Hey there." I stroked her feathered head and all the way down to the thick fur on her back. She blinked at me lazily and accepted the strip of bacon I offered to her. As she ate it, I unwrapped her bound wing and examined it. The tear the ur'gel had ripped in it had mostly healed, the skin pink and new beneath the overlapping feathers.

"I don't think you'll need this anymore." I tucked the strip of cloth into my pocket and patted her wing.

She stood and stretched her wings out to their full expanse, looking like a real-life figurehead. Her wings spanned at least six feet on each side. She took several steps backward, nudging me to the side.

"Wait, Stiarna. No. I don't think—"

But she wasn't listening to me. She took two large steps and leapt, her wings catching an updraft just before she hit the ground, pulling her up into the air. Her wings flapped, the injured one seeming to lag a bit behind the other one. But she quickly found her stride and ascended into the night sky, disappearing over the trees.

I slept soundly that night for the first time in a long time, knowing that Savarah was knocked out somewhere in another room. When I woke, it was to a face looming over me, someone's hands on my shoulders. I jerked upright, our foreheads colliding.

Arun sat back, rubbing his head. "Ow."

"What are you doing here?" I shoved his chest, but he was as immovable as a boulder.

"It's time to go. Cook is preparing our food stores. Estrid is fetching your brother. You and I need to load the supplies. Who knows when we'll be able to stock up again?"

He stood. He looked good—healthy, I meant. His shoulder was still bandaged, but the color had returned to his face. Around his neck, he wore an amulet of some sort of black stone that seemed to pulse. I caught myself staring and looked away hastily.

After he left, I dressed quickly, packing the spare set of clothes Jyne had given to me. The front courtyard was bustling with activity as the priests and kitchen staff carried supplies onto the ship. Arun was chasing some of them down, turning them away, shouting about weight limits and over-packing. I took bags from two priests and walked up the gangplank, handing them off to Arun who took them with a sigh.

Last on were Estrid and Erik, Estrid dragging him behind her, ignoring his protests. Once they were on board, Arun raised the gangplank. I stepped up to help him.

"What about Savarah?" Erik asked.

I dragged the gangplank back with Arun. With any luck, Savarah was still sound asleep and would be for the rest of the day, but I wouldn't tell Erik any of that until we were up in the air.

"Yes," called a voice from below, "what about Savarah?"

I dropped the gangplank as I whirled around, nearly crushing my toes. There, at the temple door, Savarah stood, her hands on her hips, her eyes bright. I shot a look at Estrid, who was staring at Savarah with barely concealed astonishment.

Savarah took a few steps toward the ship. "So, where are we going?"

# CHAPTER 10

Unbelievable.

Impossible.

There was no way she was awake. Not after the dose I gave her.

"You're not going anywhere," I said, my temper spiking. "Not with us."

Savarah shielded her eyes with one hand and looked up at me.

"You can stay here, or feel free to head into town to find a ship bound for Lamruil."

"Lamruil?" Savarah chuckled. "Why would I want to go to Lamruil?"

Estrid came to stand beside me at the railing. She looked casual at first, but her hand gripped the railing tight enough that her knuckles turned white. "To find Tsarra Trisfina."

"You know, the woman you said you were serving?" I reminded Savarah. Now Erik had to see—see she was a liar, that she couldn't be trusted. That she had no place among us.

"What are you talking about?" Erik had broken free from Estrid and was struggling to replace the heavy gangplank on his own. "Bring her on board." He turned to Arun. "Can't we take her to Lamruil before we search for the Valley of the Horses?"

Arun was just watching from his place behind the wheel, an amused smirk on his lips. He seemed in no rush to come to anyone's aid—ours or Savarah's. Hopefully, he would be equally disinclined to help Erik after I punched him in the face. Beside me, Estrid was balling her hands into fists, and I thought she would actually help me if it came down to beating some sense into my brother.

But instead, I took a deep breath and put a hand on her wrist. I felt her pause, too. I reminded myself this was the effect Savarah had on us, and just one more reason to keep Savarah off the ship and as far away from us as possible. Until we were gone, we had to keep our wits about us.

Which was easier said than done with Erik about to launch himself off the side of the *Duchess*. Estrid grabbed him by the back of his shirt and hauled him backward. He sprawled on the deck, blinking up at her. I skirted around them and ran for the helm. Arun watched me come with wide eyes, holding onto the wheel as if I were going to rip it from his hands. But I didn't want the wheel. I didn't care where we went, as long as we went somewhere far from here. And to do that, we first had to go up.

I didn't know much about airships, or anything really, but I knew how to at least make it do that. Skidding to a stop, I jerked on the lever beside Arun, pulling it as far as it would go.

"Frida, what—" His objection was lost in the wind as we rose quickly, and he had to grab the wheel to hold the ship steady.

Leaving the helm, I returned to the port side and leaned over the railing. Savarah was still watching us, a hand shielding her eyes. Xalph and Grissall emerged from the front door, waving and shouting their farewells, Lunla close behind them, her hands on their shoulders.

"We're going too fast!" Arun shouted, drawing my attention

from the ground to the ship, which was listing to the port side as we continued to rise so fast the wind made my eyes water.

"What can I do?" I asked, grabbing a mast as I made my way toward him. I could just imagine Savarah watching us smugly from the ground, enjoying our struggle.

He yelled something and pointed to the rope wrapped around the wooden knot next to my knee. I looked down at it, bit my lip, and jerked on the knot. It came undone and the sail overhead unfurled with a crack, drawing itself taut in a matter of seconds.

"Do the others," Arun instructed.

I slipped and slid to the next mast, passing Estrid and Erik who were wrestling on the deck. The ship rocked wildly as if it were trying to buck us off, and Erik certainly wasn't helping matters with the way he was fighting Estrid. Wind caught in our lone sail and jerked us upright. I grabbed the rear mast and undid the knot, feeling relief when the sail unfurled and filled with wind.

But it was short-lived. Having the second sail tipped us off balance, the back of the ship rising while the front of the ship dipped forward. The bowsprit clipped the top of a tree and sent us into a spin over the forest at the edge of the plateau. I launched myself forward but couldn't get my feet beneath me as I slammed into something hard. Then I was in the air, the deck spinning beneath me. Arun, still holding the wheel, reached for me, but he was too far away and getting farther away. There was nothing under me now except for the tops of trees. I was not one to give up, but if there was one thing I couldn't do, it was fly. Even I knew my limits. Sometimes.

I held my breath as I plummeted. A shadow rocketed out of the treetops. Great, if I didn't fall to my death, then I would be dinner for some dreadwing family instead. But then the light caught on the creature's golden wings and I realized it was Stiarna. The griffin passed close enough to me I could reach out and wrap my arms around her neck, abruptly turning my fall into flight. I gripped her shoulders with my knees and grabbed the feathers on her neck, my heart still pounding as my body struggled to catch up with what was happening.

The extra weight didn't slow her down. We were headed straight for the *Duchess*. The airship was still spinning out of control, rising with its rear first. Estrid was hanging from the hull nets, trying to climb her way back on board. But we didn't stop for her. I had to get that last sail opened, and Stiarna seemed to know that somehow. She took me as close as she could to the foremast, but it wasn't close enough. She had to keep a safe distance or risk getting knocked around by the ship, but because of that, there was no way I would be able to reach the rope where it was knotted.

I would have to jump, and trust that Stiarna would catch me again if I were to fall.

"Frida."

My gaze darted to the left, where Erik was pressed against the railing.

"Tell me what to do." He was panting, his eyes wide with fear, but he seemed to at least be himself.

I gave him instructions, shouting to be heard over the wind, and then Stiarna and I pulled back to watch. I was ready to jump in and get him if I needed to, but he seemed to not need my help. He made his way steadily across the deck, arms outstretched for balance. When he reached the mast, he tugged on the rope and the sail unfurled. The ship righted itself with a groan.

Estrid pulled herself over the railing and collapsed onto the deck. Stiarna landed near her and I dropped from her back, and then bent to help my sister to her feet. When she was standing, she pushed me off her and charged toward Erik, knocking him back with two hands against his chest.

"What is wrong with you?" she growled at him. "We're about

to be in our second ship wreck, and all you're worried about is that … that … witch?"

Erik grabbed her wrists. "I'm sorry."

"What?" Estrid blinked, drawn up short by his apology. It was an uncommon event, to be sure.

"It's like, when I'm with her, there's a cloud over my eyes." He still hadn't let go of her wrists, but she wasn't trying to hit him anymore.

"I know what you mean," I chimed in. "When she's near, I feel so angry."

Estrid cocked her head at me and raised an eyebrow.

"Well, angrier than usual."

"Frida and I drugged her," Estrid explained to our brother. "Last night at dinner, Frida gave her a dose of vila leaf powder that would have knocked you on your ass for at least an entire day."

I nodded. "And it didn't even last twelve hours with her."

"She can't be trusted."

Erik released Estrid and stepped away from us, running a hand through his hair. Then, to me, he asked, "Where did you get vila leaf powder?"

"Jyne, one of the young priests in the temple."

He shook his head, blinking as if stunned. "Onen help me, I would have done anything for her."

"Jyne?" I asked, taken aback.

"Savarah. Absolutely anything."

Before I could respond, a hand on my shoulder whirled me around and I came face to face with Arun. His full lips were set in a stern line, and his eyes were dark and narrowed.

"Are you okay?" I asked.

"Let me be clear," Arun said, "don't ever touch my ship again." The black amulet pulsed quickly, and I imagined it keeping time with his racing heart. He looked fine, though, given the circumstances.

I turned away, smirking, walking toward where Stiarna was grooming herself on the bow of the ship. "No one wants to touch your ship, anyway. Now, let's find us some horses." His glare burned the back of my neck, but I didn't dare turn back to him.

We flew all day, keeping the *Duchess* just below the cover of the veil so we could search the ground for any sign of horses. There were none. We did see a blazetaur nest, and a pile of shadebig bones, and once, we'd had to fight off a curious dreadwing, but there was nothing out of the ordinary. At night, when Erik and Estrid had retired to the crew's quarters below deck, and Stiarna had flown off in search of dinner, I found myself alone with Arun.

He'd been standoffish all day, quiet and brooding as he flew the ship and the rest of us shouted out tips and directions, chasing false leads across the continent. I didn't think it was that he was annoyed with our mission or still angry at me for the debacle with the ship. It was something else, something he was keeping tight-lipped about.

"Hey." I sidled up to him.

He looked at me sideways, grunted, and then returned his gaze to the night sky. We were cruising above the veil now, where it was safer, while my siblings rested.

"So, how do you know where you're going?" I asked. It wasn't that I necessarily cared, but I wanted to get him talking.

At first, it seemed like he wouldn't respond, but then he sighed and held out a hand. I put my own hand in it, and he raised it to the sky, positioning it so that the thumb and the forefinger made an L-shape. The tip of my forefinger lined up with the brightest star, and my thumb brushed the very edge of Gleet. I was more focused on his hand on mine, though. Every other time he'd touched me, his skin had been warm, almost scalding. Now, it was deathly cold.

"It's no different than sailors in ships on the sea, really," he explained. "Instead of water currents and swells, I use winds and air currents."

"And stars?"

"And stars. And Gleet. The moon is always there, even when the stars are not."

I nodded, even though none of it really made sense to me. Erik knew some of this, and since he was our leader, I'd always been content to follow him or whoever he chose to follow. Maybe it was time to learn these things, but it was hard when all I could think about was how cold and lifeless he felt. Even the dark circles beneath his eyes seemed to have returned.

"Are you okay?" I asked for the second time since boarding the ship.

He dropped my hand. "No. Not really."

I rubbed my fingers, warming them. "Is it to do with that?" I motioned toward the swirling black amulet that hung on a chain around his neck. It darkened. As if aware I was talking about it.

He lifted a hand to touch it, but let it hover over the stone instead of making contact. "This is the only thing keeping the darkness at bay."

"The darkness?"

"The dark spell that the ur'gels used to resurrect the corpses. It's inside of me. This—the piece of Lunla's soul contained inside this amulet is the only thing pushing it back."

The piece of her soul? "You mean she gave you a piece of the light?"

He shrugged. "I guess. I don't really know how it works. But I can't take it off. Strict instructions."

"What happens if you take it off?"

After a pause, he said, "I don't think I want to know."

It was hard to reconcile the man beside me with the one I'd met in the mines. The one I'd fought beside on the plateau. The one I'd walked with through the hedge maze. Now that he'd put words to it, I could see the darkness inside of him, especially in his eyes. He looked weak, angry, despondent. Not like the champion of lost causes. He *was* a lost cause.

No. I couldn't think that way. What I needed was a way to save him. A way to bring him back.

I tore my eyes away from him and tilted my head back, ready to change the subject if he was. Up here, the sky wasn't just overhead but all around us, a sea of stars. I wondered how many Svands were up here, watching me watching them. Or my mother's people—Suun or otherwise. Were they watching, too? Maybe laughing at my foolishness?

Arun shifted beside me. "What are you thinking?"

"About my family. My ancestors."

He looked thoughtfully up at the sky. "That's right. The D'ahvol believe their ancestors are in the stars."

"You don't?" The elves and the D'ahvol had such similar belief systems I'd assumed they were the same.

"It's a nice idea." He searched the skies and then pointed at a particularly bright star with a red tint to it. "That one would be Ashryn, I think."

My first instinct was to tell him it didn't work that way, but then I processed what he said. "Who?"

"Ashryn Phina, my youngest sister."

"She died?" Elves had long life spans, and death was just as rare as birth among their kind. The D'ahvol, though descended from the elves, had shorter life spans, although we still lived longer than an average human.

"Yes, when we were very young."

"Do you remember her well?" I was always curious about what others who'd lost people at a young age remembered. If they had more of their loved one than I had of my mother—the bits and pieces, glimpses of things I couldn't distinguish from true memory and a story told to me by my father.

"Yes, some things," he said. "She had fiery red hair that she wore too long, and it was always a tangled mess. She would weave grasses and flowers into the strands like some nature spirit."

I could see her in my mind's eye, though I had never met her. "What happened to her?"

"She became very sick. No one knows why, and no one could do anything about it." His hands shifted on the ship's steering wheel as we surged forward with a gust of wind. "I sat by her day and night for weeks on end. If she could have been saved by sheer force of will, I swear to you she would be with us today."

His original lost cause, I realized.

"Could it be that my parents will lose both of us to some dark sickness?"

"Don't say that." I wondered if the darkness didn't just affect his body, but his spirit, too.

"I haven't seen them in years. I left not long after Ashryn died." He laughed but there was no humor in the sound. "I tried to tell myself I was doing it to help others, but really, I was just afraid to go home. What will they think of me?" He turned his dark gaze on me. "Are they disappointed that I was the one who survived?"

"Of course not," I said, though of course I had no idea what Arun's family thought of him. I couldn't imagine my father feeling that way, though. I tried to imagine how he would feel, what he would say if I said something like that to him. "They would just be glad to have you home."

The ship rocked, and Arun turned his attention back to it, pulling on a rope to loosen one of the sails.

"What about you?" he asked after tying the rope off again. "Who do you see in the stars?"

I could lie. There were dozens of answers—my father's parents, dead before I was born. My Aunt Ragna, who died a few years ago in a dispute with an Oubliee trader. My young cousin Vott, who drowned in the waters beneath Bor'sur. But he'd told me something of substance. I could do the same. "My mother."

"I didn't realize she was dead."

I shrugged, glad he was watching the ship and the sky, and not me. "I don't know if she is or not, but I don't want to think that she left me of her own free will. Something took her from me, and I'll see her again someday, when I ride the stars at her side."

"Do you think she was killed because of her Suun heritage? Like they're hunting you now?"

"No," I said quickly. The thought honestly hadn't occurred to me before, mainly because I was so certain she wasn't descended from Onen Suun, and neither was I.

"How can you be so sure?"

It was my turn to laugh. "There is no possible way I'm the Suun heir. Saving the world is definitely not in my destiny."

"It could be."

I wasn't laughing anymore. "It's not." I knew with every part of me, inside and out, I was not the one meant to save the world from darkness. I couldn't even save one elf.

It was as if the air responded to my turmoil. The *Iron Duchess* began to shake violently, the sails beating as loud as drums against the sudden wind. A bolt of lightning below us lit the churning sea of clouds, and not a second later, thunder cracked, deafeningly loud. I cringed and grabbed the wheel to steady myself.

Arun was doing something with ropes and pulleys and paused, looking up at me.

"Take the wheel," he instructed.

"What?"

"Take it. All you have to do is hold her steady."

"Wait, no." But my hand was already on it, and when he stepped away, hauling on one of the ropes and following it to another deck, I took his place by instinct, both hands white-knuckling the spokes.

The *Duchess* was rocked by the storm. It seemed to have come out of nowhere and we were right in the middle of it. But I held on as tight as I could. Once, I loosened my grip and the wheel spun wildly. I'd gotten it quickly back under control. I caught glimpses of Arun whenever lightning illuminated the sky and the ship. He moved as fast as any crew might, running between ropes, sails, and masts, pulling, knotting, and releasing, while I stood as still as a statue, petrified of letting go.

It couldn't have lasted more than a few minutes, but it felt like forever. Eventually, we were on the other side of the storm, with nothing to show for it except for a wall of dark clouds behind us.

"You couldn't have gone around that?" I asked when Arun came back to the helm.

"Sure, I could have," he answered. "But where would be the fun in that?"

Sadly, I couldn't tell if he was joking or not. "Take your ship back."

He stood back and surveyed me, rubbing his chin as if in thought. Rain glistened on his brow and made his shirt cling to his broad chest. I did my best not to look. "I don't know," he said finally. "I don't mind the sight of you at the wheel as much as I thought I might."

"I'm going to let go."

"No, don't." He held his hands up in surrender. "But how about a lesson? Maybe you should learn. In case something does happen to me."

I wanted nothing less than to fly this ship any more than I had to. "I already told you. Don't talk like that. Nothing's going to happen to you."

"It might. Come on, just the basics."

With a few steps, he was behind me, his chest to my back, his hands covering mine on the wheel. He was saying something, lifting a hand to point at some part of the ship, but it was all nonsense to me. All I could think about was his breath, warm on my ear, and the chill of his hands on mine, all the little places where our bodies pressed together. My toes curled in my boots and I ground my teeth together. I was no better than a silly human girl melting under a man's touch. What was wrong with me? What if Erik or Estrid walked out now and saw us? I would never live it down.

I turned my head to try to look at him, so I could object, push him away, but instead, I caught a glimpse of the amulet around his neck. The black gem was pulsing quickly, truly keeping time, I realized, with his racing heart. I swallowed, trying extremely hard to keep my composure.

He had an amulet to keep his darkness at bay, but what about me? What did I have to keep my own shadows at a distance? Nothing but my dignity and the walls I put up around myself.

With every ounce of self-control I possessed, I ducked beneath his arm and freed myself from the cage he'd made for me out of his body. He stopped talking and blinked at me where I stood a few paces away now. I was safely out of his reach, and he was out of mine. And it was a good thing, too, because some irrational part of my brain wanted me to reach out and run my fingers through his wind-blown hair.

"For the last time, nothing is going to happen to you." I took another step back just to be safe, and rested my hand on the ax handle at my hip. "I don't want to learn how to fly the ship because I don't need to. Because you'll be doing it."

He didn't say anything else as I turned away and left the helm, descending onto the lower deck just as Stiarna touched down. I sat on a crate and she curled beside me. Her back and wings were wet with rain. I rubbed her, drying her with my hands. When that was done, I curled into her warmth, my head on her shoulder. She purred, a low rumble against me. All the while, I felt Arun's eyes on me and forced myself to keep looking forward at the sky ahead, a sky that felt strangely less like an ocean and more like a black hole where I might lose myself.

# CHAPTER 12

"Horses!"

The shout jerked me into consciousness. Stiarna had curled around me, and she shifted when I sat up, clucking with irritation. The sun had risen while I'd slept, and I squinted in the sudden brightness.

"Where?" There was the thunder of footsteps as someone raced to the starboard railing.

I stood quickly, rubbing the sleep from my eyes. Estrid and Erik were just to my left, leaning against the railing, while Arun stood at the helm where I'd left him, a hand over his eyes as he tried to see what they saw. I crossed to the rail and leaned over.

We were below the veil, flying over a field situated between two plateaus, rocky cliff faces reaching for the ship. The field was dotted with large tawny animals, their necks sloping toward the ground. Stiarna leapt onto the bow and began to pace back and forth in the small space. One of the horses looked up, sounded a whinny of alarm, and they all bolted, kicking up dust as they ran from our shadow.

"Unbelievable." Erik pushed off the railing and turned to Arun. "Bring her around. Let's see what this is all about."

Arun nodded and began barking orders at the three of us, no matter that we didn't know half of what he was saying. Erik clearly had a better understanding than Estrid and I though, and he dragged Estrid toward the mast where they began fiddling with the sails again.

I joined them, picking up the end of a rope.

Estrid took it from me. "Don't worry, we've got it." She glanced at me, then away, back to her work.

No, she hadn't looked at me. She'd looked at the star beside my eye.

"What are you talking about?" I took the rope back from her and began working at the knot as she had been. "Just tell me what to do."

She jerked it from my grasp, harder this time. "It's fine. We don't—" She caught herself.

I put a hand on my hip. "Don't what?"

"Come on, let's move," Arun shouted from the helm.

Erik huffed and walked away, not looking back at me.

"Don't what?" I repeated.

Her voice was nearly a whisper when she said, "Need you."

Apparently, the bond we'd reformed over our mutual mistrust of Savarah had been forgotten, and I was back to being the odd one out. But not just out this time. Different. Special.

"I didn't mean it like that," she added, but not quickly enough.

"I'm not the Suun heir." I ran a hand through my hair and ignored Arun, who was shouting at us. "You guys think I'm running all over this island because I think I'm destined to save the world?"

She shrugged noncommittally.

"You said it yourself. My mother didn't have the mark. Father doesn't either. There's no way I'm descended from Onen Suun."

"Then why are we doing this?" She waved her hands around to encompass everything—the ship and the search.

"Because if I go home now, I bring this danger with me. I want to clear my name and keep my family safe." I couldn't bring walking corpses and ur'gels with me back to Bor'sur. I didn't want to save the world, but I did want to save the people I loved. That, at least, I knew I could do. *That,* I thought, *could be my true destiny.*

We were distracted by Erik's shout, and both of us rushed to help him and Arun bring the ship down into a clearing. The mountains around us were the rocky cliffs to which we were accustomed, but the valley itself was a lush, green field cut in two by a small, winding river. It was peaceful, which was definitely not the Bruhier standard.

As soon as the ship touched down, Stiarna leapt from the bow and darted away, the arch of her wings the only thing visible over the tall grass. I followed, scrambling down the hull nets, not waiting for the gangplank. I wasn't entirely sure it was a good idea to put down the gangplank. It was like Xalph had said: Bruhier could be a tricky place. Safety was often an illusion, so I would be the first to check it out.

I shuffled through the grass all the way to the bank of the river. It was not very wide and did not look very deep. I stooped and dipped my fingers in, letting the cool water rush over my hand.

Arun knelt beside me, scooping a handful of water to his mouth and sipping before I could object. I worried it would be awkward between us, but he made no mention of what had passed between us the night before. He smacked his lips and stood, his hands on his hips. "So, where are the monsters?"

It was exactly what I had been wondering, though I had not been quite so eager to speak the words. But there was also something else. "Where are the horses?"

"They came this way," he said, looking around as if they were hiding somewhere nearby. There was nowhere for them to hide, though.

"Should we look for them?"

"I think we're supposed to look for the Sisters of Light."

"Do you think they're with the horses?"

I had no idea, but I wouldn't tell him that. I was the reason we were on this wild goose chase in the first place. It was time to start at least pretending like I knew what was going on. Instead of answering, I stood up and spun around, taking in my surroundings. If I were to put a temple here, where would it be? But my eyes kept drifting to the cliffs, to the plateaus above the veil. I couldn't imagine trying to live down here, even if there were no obvious threats.

"I guess we should start looking," I said finally, not able to come up with a better answer. "We might need to go up."

"We might. Let's get Erik and—"

"Frida!"

Both of us turned toward the ship where Erik and Estrid had stayed to keep watch. They were standing there now, waving their arms frantically over their heads and shouting something incoherent.

"What?" I shouted back.

Erik started making motions with his hands as if beckoning us toward him.

"I don't like this," Arun said slowly.

"Maybe they found something. The temple."

Arun tapped on my shoulder and pointed past me. "Or the horses."

I followed his finger. Across the river, a huge horse watched us, its fur-tufted ears pressed back against its neck. It was taller than any horse I'd ever seen, easily towering over both Arun and me. There was more movement further downstream and another horse appeared. There was something different about these horses, something I couldn't quite put my finger on. They were tall and slender, all sleek muscles and angles. Sharp was the word that came to mind. When the second horse bared its teeth at us, I knew why. These were no normal horses, no docile creatures for riding and plowing fields.

The reason there were no monsters in this valley was because the horses *were* the monsters.

Its teeth were sharp points, like fangs for ripping apart meat. It reared, and I saw its hooves were clawed instead of round. When its feet touched the ground, it snorted, and I could have sworn I saw smoke come out of its nostrils.

What were these things?

Arun shoved my arm, turning me around, pushing me toward the ship. "Run."

We ran. There was no sound except for the swishing of the grass beneath our feet and our steady breaths. Then came the splashing. I made the mistake of turning around and nearly fell. Dozens of horses were emerging from the tree line on the other side of the river. They were wading through the water and charging up the bank where we'd been standing moments before. I stumbled over my own feet, but Arun's hand on my upper arm kept me upright.

"Get ready," Arun shouted at my siblings, who were still standing there waving and shouting at us. "Get ready to fly!"

Both of them scrambled out of view, presumably to prepare the ship for takeoff.

The small distance between us and the ship seemed to grow as we ran, and I wondered if this was another one of Bruhier's tricks. The lead horse was right behind me, so close I could hear it snorting as it ran. Its teeth grazed my shoulder and I braced myself, ready to be mauled, trampled, or a combination of both.

But just then, a dark shape bounded out of the grass, running sideways at me, and ran headlong into the beast. They collided with a snarl and a grunt. I glanced over my shoulder to see Stiarna scrabbling with the horse, stamping down the grass as they rolled. The horse had the advantage of its size, but Stiarna was agile. The horse was on his back, snapping its teeth wildly, but Stiarna seemed to be avoiding the fangs.

I hesitated, my hand on my ax, debating whether or not to help her.

"Come on," Arun said breathlessly, passing me, dragging me behind him.

The gangplank came into view finally. Erik and Estrid waved us on from the top, where they stood ready to pull it in. We hit the ramp at a run. I stopped to help them bring in the gangplank, forgetting our earlier argument about them not needing my help anymore. They certainly didn't send me away, not with the herd bearing down on us. When it was in, I searched the grass for Stiarna, but she was nowhere to be seen beneath the sea of horses charging toward the ship.

Arun was at the helm, chanting, "Up, up, up," but we weren't moving.

"Um, Arun?" I said.

He didn't respond but kept muttering to himself as he rushed around tugging on ropes and sails.

The first horse reached the ship, but it didn't stop. It crashed into the wood, making the deck tremble. I grabbed the railing to stay on my feet as more and more horses reached us. The force of their impact rocked the ship, carving a deep groove in the dirt beneath us as the ship shifted.

"Now, Arun!" I shouted, all semblance of calm gone.

Still not acknowledging me, he pulled the lever beside the wheel up gradually, not in a panic as I had done the day before.

Erik, who stood beside me, grimaced as the ship shook and shifted again. "I think they want us out of their valley."

I nodded, but my attention had been drawn back to the grass and the river beyond, and a dark wing rising from the grass.

"Stiarna," I said to no one in particular.

The ship rose a few feet off the ground only to be shoved by the horses. I went to my knees as the ship rocked and touched down again. Through the bars of the railing, I watched the same thing happen to Stiarna—she got a few feet off the ground, only to be dragged back down by a horse pulling on her wing.

I shouted for her. Erik shouted for Arun. Arun shouted for us all to shut up.

And finally, the *Iron Duchess* got out of reach of the stampeding horses and began to rise steadily. Stiarna gave a mighty flap, kicked the horse that had ahold of her in the muzzle, and soared into the sky.

I gave a sigh of relief and collapsed against the railing. We were safe, all of us, even if we were no closer to the Sisters of Light.

CHAPTER 13

We were safe, but only as long as we stayed in the
air. On the ground, the horses were trailing us,
screaming at us as they kicked up dirt and dust. It
was like being followed by a storm, if storms had teeth. Stiarna
flew beside us, and I was pretty sure she stayed visible just to
taunt them. Her only wounds from the fight were some superficial scratches. For that, and for her safety, I was grateful.

As we circled this part of the island, it became clear the
horses wouldn't follow us into the trees that crept up the
foothills. They seemed to keep to the confines of the field.

"What are we going to do?" I asked finally.

Arun peered over the ship's edge, keeping his hands on the
wheel. "I can't land in the jungle."

He looked worse after our encounter with the horses. His
eyes were sunken into his face and he couldn't seem to catch his
breath. The amulet around his neck was almost completely
black now, and it pulsed slower than it seemed it should. Slower
than a heart should beat, if that was, in fact, what it was keeping
time with. He was changing, dying, and I didn't know how to
stop it. I didn't know how to save him, not without the Sisters

of Light. And it was quickly becoming evident we wouldn't find the Sisters of Light from up here.

"Well, we have to land somewhere," I said.

Estrid looked at me like she wanted to make some smart remark about me giving orders, but she didn't. Just another example of how she'd changed around me. Before she thought I was the Suun heir, she never would have held back.

Arun either didn't notice the tension between me and my sister, or he ignored it. "There is something I could try. I could bring her down in the trees."

Erik narrowed his eyes. "What do you mean, 'in the trees'?"

"In the branches," Arun explained. "So that we're not on the ground, and I don't have to find a field large enough to hold the *Duchess*."

"Have you done that before?" I asked. I had just gotten used to the idea of flying ships, and now he wanted to put one in a tree.

"No, but I've been thinking about it. See that tree over there?" He pointed, and we all followed his finger to one of the taller trees at the base of a nearby mountain. Its branches were thick and likely sturdy, and widespread, like arms pushing its neighbors away, creating a lot of space around it. Enough space for a ship.

"And we would what? Climb down?"

"Yes."

"What if it doesn't work?" Estrid asked, always the one to look at all the possibilities. "What if the ship falls?"

Arun looked at me finally, as if I had been the one to ask the question. "Then we fall. And we'll have no way out of the valley except to climb."

"Have you seen a town or anywhere we can go in case that happens?" I didn't like the idea of finding another Barepost, but I liked the idea of wandering around Bruhier without a plan and help even less.

But Arun shook his head. "The only other thing would be to go back to the temple."

Go back to the temple and admit defeat. Go back to the temple and let Arun die. And let others suffer because I couldn't prove the truth of who I was. "No. That's not an option."

"I didn't think so."

We left the horses in the field and made our way over to the tree, watching for any sign of being followed and seeing none. Arun brought the ship down slowly, guided by Erik who ran back and forth to make sure we were positioned just right, while Estrid and I held our breath and manned the sails just in case. The tree groaned as the *Duchess* settled in, but it held. When Arun announced the flying mechanism was off and we'd docked, we all cheered.

The climb down the tree was slow and tedious without our climbing gear, which we'd left back at the temple, thinking we'd have no need for it. Who needed to climb trees or mountains when they had a flying ship, right? The Svands, that's who. I was relieved but immediately on guard when my feet touched the ground. The four of us stood in a silent crowd, standing close together as if that alone might ward off any threat.

Estrid was beside me, also alert. "What is it?" she asked.

"I don't know. It's so ... quiet." Stiarna had stayed behind on the ship, sleeping and recovering from her recent fight, so we didn't have her innate sense of danger to guide us. Still, even I could tell something was wrong. I didn't hear any birds or the rustle of small creatures in the brush. Not even the wind swept through the branches.

That was why the crack of a branch behind us was loud enough to be nearly deafening. We whirled as one and came face to face with a shadebig. Movement in the shadows revealed more of them, staring at us with pale, blank eyes from the cover of the surrounding trees.

"Hm." I nodded once and drew my ax, unable to take my eyes

from its fearful form. "This must be why the horses stay out of the forest."

We'd encountered these monsters before in the area around Barepost, and it had never been a fun experience. We still weren't sure entirely what they were. They looked like a human who had taken body parts from other animals and sewn them together, wearing them like a suit. Deer heads with sharpened antlers, human torsos with exposed bone, and hind legs of a goat. It was gruesome and terrifying. And to make matters worse, we still didn't know how to kill them.

One of them lunged at Estrid. She took a swing at its outstretched arm and sliced it off at the elbow. The arm fell twitching to the ground, and from the stump, another limb sprouted.

"I remember this," Estrid said drily.

Arun cursed. He had his bow and arrow, but I didn't know what good they would be against these monsters. Then again, my ax apparently wasn't going to be of much use either, not if they just grew back whatever I managed to slice off.

When one charged at me, I didn't have time to think about it anymore. It ran on two feet in a strange, loping gallop, its too-long arms flopping beside it. It would have been almost comical if not for the fact its torso was torn open and I could see its heart beating, blood oozing from the gaping hole that didn't slow it down at all. My ax glanced off its armored skull and one of its bone-white antlers shoved against my shoulders, pushing me back into Arun. He caught me with one hand, and reached around me with the other, driving an arrow into the monster's eye. The thing shrieked, a sound terrible enough I nearly covered my ears. Instead, I swung my ax at its neck, severing its head and silencing it.

But not for good. Arun and I watched in horror as a new head, just as hideous, popped out of the creature's neck stump. I looked down to make sure the other head was still there. It was, complete with Arun's arrow sticking out of the eye socket.

Grunting, I shoved the shadebig back. It stumbled, arms flailing. I hooked my ax around its knee and it fell to the ground. I hacked at its face, its neck, its shoulder, blood splattering me and the ground around us. It was gruesome, and maybe unnecessary, but I was so done with this place. Done with Bruhier and its monsters that wouldn't die. I just wanted to be left alone to find the Sisters of Light, to save my friend, to save my family. I didn't need this shit.

When it was sufficiently hacked up to the point where it would take it at least a few minutes to regenerate, I stood up, panting, and looked for the others. Estrid and Erik were holding their own, fighting back-to-back and holding off the pack. Arun, though, was not faring so well. He was pressed against the tree, struggling with a shadebig who had its claws around his neck.

I grabbed the creature's shoulders and jerked it back. It released Arun and turned on me instead, which was just fine. Arun looked awful, like he could just fall down dead at any moment. The amulet around his neck was almost solid black, the pulsing barely visible.

The shadebig fell backward on top of me, plastering me to the ground. I thrashed and struggled beneath its substantial weight as it tried to roll over and get its hands around my neck instead. It had very nearly succeeded when a blade flashed in front of my face and severed its head. Hot blood poured over my chest and neck. I gagged and pulled myself out from beneath the creature before it could get itself together.

Estrid stood over me, a hand held out to help me up.

"Thanks." I took her hand and let her pull me to my feet.

The shadebigs were still coming. Those that had fallen were regenerating, and the others were circling, waiting for their comrades.

"We should get back up the tree," Estrid said, pushing me forward to where Erik and Arun were already waiting.

They linked their fingers together and Estrid stepped into the cradle of their hands. With her other leg, she pushed off the ground and they heaved her up, her fingers grasping for the lowest branch. Grasping and missing.

Estrid stumbled back to the ground. "I can't reach it."

I stepped up. "Try me."

A shadebig had made a move and Estrid was forcing it back. She took off its arms with two blows of her sword and finally, its head. The body collapsed to the ground, but we all knew it wouldn't stay there.

"You should hurry," Estrid urged.

But there was no time to get into position. The shadebigs were closing in on us again, and this time had us surrounded.

"Frida, climb on my shoulders," Erik said, holding his sword in one hand and his shield in the other. "You can make it."

"I won't leave you." I couldn't even believe he thought I would.

"It's the only—"

"Shh!" Estrid cut off his protest with a sharp sound that quieted us. "What's that sound?"

There was a steady pounding I not only heard, but also felt in my feet. Almost like… "Galloping?" I squinted into the shadows of the forest. "Horses?"

Arun cursed again. None of us had anything to add.

But then there was something else—a light. And just as my brain processed what I was seeing, a woman on horseback burst out of the trees, brandishing a glowing sword over her head. With a battle cry, she barreled down on the shadebigs, her sword slicing cleanly through two of them at once. They fell, and this time, they didn't stir. The four of us stood in open-mouthed wonder, watching her dispatch one after another. The shadebigs seemed just as astonished, barely fighting back. Even more impressive was she was doing this all from the back of one of the monster horses.

I huddled close to my siblings and Arun, letting the woman work. The horse wove expertly around the trees while she cut down the shadebigs until finally, none were left standing. It was a massacre, a circle of mutilated bodies and blood-soaked ground, and we were in the middle of it. She stopped a few feet from us and surveyed her work. The glowing sword rested across one thigh.

When it became evident no one else would, I took a step forward to speak. But before I could, she wheeled the horse on me and leveled the blade at my throat, though I was more concerned with the horse's gnashing teeth inches from my face. Not one to back down, I bared my teeth at the beast. In response, it snorted smoke at me. I coughed and waved away the cloud.

"Tell me who you are," she demanded, her blue eyes blazing down the length of the sword. "Be warned that if I do not like the answer, you will meet the monster's same fate."

# CHAPTER 14

The D'ahvol spent our entire lives either fighting or training to fight. Weapons became an extension of our limbs, a constant presence from the time we were old enough to walk. Erik, Estrid, and I were no exception. When I'd been born, Erik had carved an ax out of the wood from a river birch I'd carried around and even slept with for years, until my father gave me the ax I had now. It was my greatest treasure, the head made of iron and steel and the hilt carved with my name in Ahvoli runes. Erik and Estrid had chosen the more traditional swords, and I'd grown up with the ringing of their wooden practice swords as my constant lullaby.

That was why, when this woman lowered her sword at me, I wasn't afraid.

I was astonished.

She was small, with delicate features and thin arms beneath a lightweight dress. She was dressed in the orange robes of a priest. But she fought like a warrior and controlled the horse-beast as if she were ten times its size.

"How did you do that?" I asked instead of answering the question she'd leveled at me.

She looked at one of the bodies that had fallen nearest to us. It was cleaved in half from its shoulder to its waist, oozing red blood in a puddle that nearly reached my boot. "Everyone in this area knows that in order to kill a shadebig, one must have an iron sword that's been dipped in the Lake of Light."

"Oh," Estrid said, "of course," though she certainly had no more idea what the woman was talking about than I did. When she saw me glaring at her, she smirked and subtly pinched my arm.

I decided to ignore her. "And what, exactly, is the Lake of Light?" I'd never heard of it but that didn't mean much, especially if it was as obscure as the Sisters of Light.

The girl seemed to remember herself. She put the sword back to my throat and glowered, as if it were my fault she'd forgotten to kill me. "That's not important. Who are you, and why are you here?"

What could we say? I still didn't know if she was friend or foe. She'd saved us from the shadebigs, but only to hold us at sword point. I brushed my hair back from my face, tucking it behind my ears as I considered my answer.

If I hadn't been watching her, I would have missed it. The furrowed brow as she caught sight of the star beside my eye. She pushed my chin with the sword, turning my head slightly to the left to get a better look. Then, more carefully, her voice low and careful, she asked again, "Who are you?"

"We've been sent by Lunla," I said. Then, I added on a whim, "We're friends of Beru." I didn't know what made me say it—maybe the way she'd looked at the star and been more intrigued than curious—but it seemed to work.

Her eyebrows came together, she opened her mouth, snapped it shut, and opened it again, sucking in a breath. But before she could ask whatever question she was formulating, there was a crash in the trees not far away. All our heads turned toward the sound, but nothing emerged.

"It isn't safe here." The girl began to turn the horse with what seemed to be just a squeeze of her legs. "Follow me." She turned and passed between two trees without looking back.

We all stood and watched her, unmoving, barely even breathing.

"Who is she?" Arun asked with maybe a little too much amazement in his voice.

I looked away from him before I could roll my eyes. "Do we go?"

Erik shrugged. "What choice do we have?"

Estrid also watched the woman's retreating back. "If she's from around here, maybe she can help us find the Sisters of Light."

I guessed they were right. Getting back in the ship would put us right back at square one. And Arun looked worse, leaning against the tree as if barely able to stand without its support. I wondered about the Lake of Light, and if it perhaps was what he needed to chase away the darkness.

Just as we were deciding, the woman glanced back over her shoulder at us. "Or you can stay and tangle with the next pack of shadebigs coming this way. They won't be pleased to see their friends torn to pieces."

None of us were too eager for that. I followed, Estrid behind me, and Erik bringing up the rear, Arun leaning on him heavily. The forest seemed to get larger in scale as we went, or we were shrinking. The trees became wider and taller. The underbrush had berries as big as my fist and leaves as big as my head. The horse-beast cut a confident path through the growing woods, and we followed, careful not to stray too far. If the trees were bigger, what did that mean for the animals?

We did not walk long before the woman slowed, the rest of us stopping behind her.

"What is it?" Estrid asked.

"We're here." The woman slid sideways off the horse, which stood docile and patient.

I looked around. I'd expected a clearing, a garden, and a towering stone temple like Lunla's. But there was nothing here. Just more giant trees and the same unsettling stillness. I put my hand on the trunk of the tree beside me. I barely came up past where its roots met its base. It was enormous, big enough around I assumed this must be what it was like to be a bug.

The woman shouldered past me and approached what I hadn't seen before—a door at the base of the tree, not concealed, necessarily, but barely visible, made of the bark of the tree with a small groove for a handle. I was relieved to see it was of a normal size. She put her hand to the door and it pulsed with light so briefly I would have missed it if I'd blinked. Then she pulled on the handle and it opened outward.

"This way," she said, disappearing inside. The horse-beast followed her, barely fitting through the opening.

Not one to be outdone by the animal, I went next. But I'd been wholly unprepared for what waited for us on the other side.

I'd expected a crude hideaway inside a hollowed-out tree, but that was not what I got. We were standing inside a temple almost identical to Lunla's, though more jewel-toned than gold. The ceilings were high overhead, held up by wooden columns which had been carved to look like different Bruhier monsters in all their terrifying glory and polished to a high shine. The same pews stretched ahead in two rows, but instead of stone benches, these seemed to be molded out of the wood of the tree and growing right out of the floor.

"Wow," Estrid muttered.

She wasn't wrong.

Arun dropped into one of the pews, which creaked under his weight.

The woman stopped a few yards away and turned, holding her arms out wide. "Welcome," she said proudly, "to the Temple of Light."

# CHAPTER 15

"Tell me about your connection to Beru Halsted."

I hadn't even known that was his surname, but I didn't let the surprise show on my face. Instead, I dropped my eyes to the bowl in front of me while I considered my answer.

We were gathered around a large wooden dining table that, just like the benches, was a part of the tree itself. The priest, who had introduced herself as Ravyn, had to have tremendous elemental magic to be able to maintain this place, even if she wasn't the one who had created it. It was possible there was someone else here who had earth magic, but we hadn't seen anyone else since we'd walked inside. It was a far cry from Lunla's temple, which had priests and priests-in-training in every room. I supposed it wasn't in a very desirable location, but I couldn't imagine her being here alone.

Ravyn had even been the one to serve us our meal, a thin stew with more root vegetables than meat. It made Gerves's special stew he always made from the previous day's leftovers look good, but we were all eating happily, none of us picky eaters.

"We met Beru outside of Barepost," I said finally, not sure what part of the story to give her.

"Here, on Bruhier? How is that possible? He is supposed to be…"

"Imprisoned in the Barren Wastes? A dreamwalker broke him out. A girl called Aria. who was traveling with him."

Ravyn nodded, her eyes flicking from side to side before landing back on me. "Does that have anything to do with rumors of the ur'gels attacking the area?"

"They're not just rumors," Estrid interjected. She'd nearly cleaned her bowl and was wiping the sides with a slice of soft bread. "We've fought them ourselves. They're looking for her." She pointed the bread at me accusingly.

"Wait a minute," I started, but Ravyn jumped in.

"Because you bear the mark the Creator bestowed on Onen Suun."

I nodded, noting she had not said I was his heir, only that I bore his mark. "When she released Beru from the prison, she created a crack in the spell that is growing, releasing more and more of the darkness back into the world. Beru thought that I was some sort of key to keeping the prison closed."

"And he told you to come to the Valley of the Horses?"

"No," I corrected her, "Lunla did. There was an ur'gel attack on her temple and Arun saved her life." I gestured at the elf, who was staring down into his bowl. He wasn't eating and apparently not listening either, because he didn't glance up. "In exchange, she gave us this one hint: to seek the Sisters of Light, in the Valley of the Horses."

"She did not accompany you?" Ravyn asked, her own bowl of stew untouched.

I took a spoonful of stew and swallowed before answering. "No. She stayed behind. We left her a couple of our younger traveling companions."

"And Savarah," Erik said almost longingly. I wanted to

launch the rest of my bowl across the table at him, but Ravyn's reaction stilled my hand.

Her head whipped toward my brother, her stare intense. "What name did you say?"

"Savarah," he repeated.

"Tell me she has not also been released."

"Released from what?" Erik asked cluelessly.

But I saw immediately what she was saying, and everything clicked into place. Savarah wasn't just manipulative and cruel, she was evil. Evil enough that Onen Suun had locked her away in an eternal prison with the Dark One and all his minions.

"Who was she?" I asked.

Across the table, Estrid leaned over to whisper in Erik's ear, likely filling him in on what he was still too blind to see for himself. Savarah had really done a number on our brother.

Ravyn linked her fingers together and tapped them against her chin before beginning. "Beru Halsted had once been one of Onen Suun's finest and most trusted lieutenants. To Onen Suun's despair, he was thought to be killed in one of the most horrific battles of the Dark War, just a few days before Onen Suun sacrificed himself and the high dragons in order to create the prison in which Dag'draath now resides."

"But he wasn't dead," Estrid chimed in.

"He wasn't dead. He'd been captured, and because he'd been with Dag'draath's troops when the walls went up, he was trapped there as well, and so were Dag'draath's lieutenants. Of them, Savarah was perhaps his most trusted."

"Why?" I asked breathlessly. I felt validated and couldn't wait to gloat to Erik and Estrid later that all my suspicions about Savarah had been right after all. Maybe it wouldn't kill them to listen to me every now and then. Maybe, just maybe, it would save their lives.

"Because she proved her loyalty to him by betraying Onen Suun, although, to be fair, Onen Suun had betrayed her first."

"You mean she loved him?"

"She wanted him. Whether or not it was love is not for me to judge. But when he did not return her affection, she hurt him in the worst way she knew how."

"By going to the dark side."

Ravyn nodded. "By loving his enemy and using her powers for evil."

"Her powers?" Erik leaned forward.

"She's an empath, with the power to influence the moods of those around her. You can see how that would have been helpful in battle."

Sure. Send in one person to convince the other side that they don't want to fight and save thousands of lives. But send in one person to stir things up, to brew anger and fuel grudges, and it would be bloodshed and chaos. The kind of chaos the Dark War had thrived on. It also explained why everyone around her was always at odds. Why my siblings and I hadn't been getting along ever since she arrived in Barepost with Tsarra Trisfina.

Ravyn looked at each of us in turn, her solemn gaze lingering lastly on Erik. "Heed my warning: stay away from Savarah. She is one of Dag'draath's greatest weapons."

Arun, who had been unusually quiet through the whole conversation, gave a low moan.

"Arun?" I leaned forward to try to look at his face.

When he turned toward me, his eyes were as black as the amulet around his neck, and he lunged, teeth bared.

# CHAPTER 16

A run's hands wrapped around my neck and the momentum propelled us both backward out of our chairs. We crashed to the floor, wood splintering beneath us. He gnashed his teeth just inches from my face, but I held him back with my arms against his chest.

"Arun, stop," I choked out.

But it wasn't Arun above me. It was someone else—*something* else. And whatever it was, it wasn't listening to me.

I kicked and bucked my hips, but he was deadweight, pressing me against the wooden floor. His hands pressed tighter against my windpipe. There was the scraping of chairs and raised voices, but it all grew increasingly faint, as if Arun and I had left the world behind. It was just the two of us and whatever darkness occupied his broken mind.

Then, there was a strange cracking sound, like splitting wood, and suddenly I could breathe again. Arun dangled over me, his arms pinned to his side by winding branches. Behind him, an ancient face made of peeling white and brown tree bark leered at me.

I blinked, scrambled back, and fumbled for the ax at my

waist. But before I could draw it, Ravyn put herself between me and the tree monster.

"Do not draw your weapon," she said. "Eoghan is my servant."

So, she wasn't here alone after all.

Estrid appeared behind me and pulled me to my feet, but I didn't take my eyes off the tree monster. It was almost exactly like the one we had fought on the cliffs above Barepost, though maybe a bit smaller. And not trying to kill us.

"What is he?" Erik asked. He was the only one of us with the nerve to approach Eoghan, and he stood below him now, running a hand along the bark of what seemed to be a leg. Arun dangled placidly a few feet above Erik's head, all the fight seeming to have left him. Erik ignored him.

"He's a trehand, one of the most ancient beings on this island." Ravyn looked up at her servant with what could only be admiration. "They are typically peaceful creatures that are not commonly seen, though they are always around us. They will sleep for centuries until called to awaken."

It was strange for me to see this creature as more than a monster. "Why is Eoghan awake?" I asked.

Ravyn smiled. "Eoghan is a curious trehand. He and a few others have been my companions since I arrived at the temple. I believe the light sent them to me, to keep me company in what would otherwise be a lonely existence. It likely helps I am a powerful earth elemental."

She approached Eoghan and its captive then and gestured for the trehand to lower Arun to her level. It obeyed. Arun's head lolled forward, lifeless. Ravyn peeled back one of his eyelids, then the other, and put her fingers to the amulet around his neck. A visible chill went through her body.

"This looks like the work of Savarah," Ravyn said.

"No." Estrid shook her head. "This was the ur'gels."

I elbowed her. "Who was with the ur'gels when the walking corpses were dropped on our heads?"

She huffed a sigh. "Savarah."

"Exactly. It seems to make sense it was all her doing. The ur'gels may have some intelligence, but enough to pull this off?" I gestured at Arun.

Ravyn walked away, slinging a cloak over her shoulders. "We must get to the Lake of Light before nightfall," she said to no one in particular. "And before he is taken again."

Taken. That seemed to be a good description for what had happened to Arun. I hadn't realized how close he'd been to the darkness, how tightly he'd been holding on for our sakes. For my sake? Anyone else might have given him up for lost, but he was the champion of lost causes, and now it was my turn to be his.

"Let's go," I ordered my siblings, ushering them behind Ravyn and Eoghan.

Instead of leaving the way we'd come in, we went out a back door beside the quiet kitchen in the depths of the temple. All of us, especially Eoghan, had to duck low to fit through the small door. We emerged beneath a midday sky, the sun directly over-head and shining brightly through the thin veil of a beautiful day. I thought, not for the first time, how strange it was that such horrors existed alongside such beauty in this world.

I found myself beside Ravyn, who walked quickly behind Eoghan, her head down, her face determined. Taking advantage of her companionship, I asked, "So, can you tell me more about the Suun heir?"

"The Suun heir," Ravyn began, "the key to the prison. The savior of the world. I can see why you wouldn't want it to be you."

"It isn't me."

She made a noise low in her throat that was neither agree-ment nor dissent. "I cannot tell you much about the Suun heir. I can tell you as long as you are here, you are safe. Let us heal your elf, and then you and your friends can decide the next steps."

"He's not my—"

My objection died on my lips when we emerged from the thick forest onto the banks of a small lake. It wasn't the lake that took my words, but the darkness. I'd thought at first that perhaps the veil had blocked out the sun, but when I looked up, I saw the truth. The trees that lined the banks had reached across toward each other, their branches intertwining and creating a dome of protection over the water. That alone made it clear this was no ordinary lake. It also explained why we hadn't seen it from the air. I wondered if they were all tree monsters, or trehands.

Ravyn knelt beside it and dipped her fingers into the water. A ring of light rippled away from her fingers, and soon, the entire lake was ablaze with it. It cast a strange reflection on the leaves above, giving us the illusion of being in an upside place.

She gestured to Eoghan. "Go on, then."

The trehand proceeded to walk into the water, Arun still in his arms. He had begun to struggle, but Eoghan held tight, not seeming to even notice.

"What will happen to him?" I asked.

Ravyn watched them as she answered. "Nothing evil can exist in the Lake of Light. The waters will purge the darkness from him. If there is enough light left inside of him, he will survive."

I turned to her, startled. "And if there isn't?"

"Then he will perish."

"Wait a minute." I started to walk forward after Eoghan, but Ravyn stopped me with an iron grip on my arm.

"You enter those waters at your own peril. Do you believe you are pure enough of soul?"

I noticed that Erik and Estrid hung far back, and even Ravyn had not touched the lake again. Only Eoghan entered without hesitation, and it made me wonder at my definition of monster.

Eoghan carried Arun to the very middle of the lake, where the water came up past its legs, and began to lower Arun into the water. When the first drop touched Arun's feet, his eyes opened, the black orbs blank. He growled and clawed at Eoghan, dragging his nails along the bark. When the trehand was unaffected, Arun then began to try to climb, his movements rigid and inhuman, as if he'd forgotten how to use his limbs. But Eoghan did not relent, finally freeing himself from Arun's panic and plunging the elf into the water.

I stepped as close as I dared to the water's edge, but everyone else stood perfectly still, even Eoghan. I imaged even the trees around us were watching, waiting to see if he would reemerge. The thought he wouldn't made me feel physically sick and I pressed a hand to my heart to try to slow its beating. Estrid must have seen it, because she came up behind me then and wrapped her arms around my shoulders.

"He'll be fine," she whispered.

But would he? What did I really know about him? I knew that when he loved someone, he loved them fiercely and with his entire heart. He was loyal, and trusting, and loved the wind on his face and the freedom of flying. He was terrible at mazes and looked good with his shirt off. I also knew if we were to discover I was truly the Suun heir, he would never, ever make me feel unworthy of the title. But did any of that make him stronger than the darkness Savarah had planted inside of him?

I made a quick, silent appeal to Zoe, the goddess of life. Let him live. Let him live and I would admit that he was my elf after all.

Arun burst through the surface, gasping for breath. Eoghan scooped him out of the water. Too stunned to fight it, Arun collapsed against the trehand. I felt the same, tipping back against my sister who kept me upright with a hand to my back.

"I told you," she said.

We moved to the side to let Eoghan pass, carrying a dripping Arun in his long-limbed arms. He looked dead. If I hadn't seen him open his eyes and take a breath just moments before, I would have assumed he'd drowned. There was a lock of dark hair across his face leaving a trail of water across his lips.

Erik appeared beside us. "Incredible."

The three of us walked together behind Eoghan and Ravyn on the way back to the temple. It felt strangely like the old times, traipsing through the woods with them, yet still very different. We weren't hunting monsters, not anymore. Now we were hunting for something else. Something much more dangerous.

"I feel I must apologize," Erik said eventually, stepping aside to hold back a branch for us.

Estrid and I passed, shooting confused glances at each other as we paused and waited for him.

"Especially to you, Frida." He nodded at me.

"For what?" I asked.

We were walking again, but he slowed to put more distance between us and the priest. "For not listening to you when you tried to tell me about Savarah. For insisting on taking her with us. For fighting you every step of the way."

I never in a million years thought I would hear Erik apologize to me for not listening to me. It was just something I was used to. But he was obviously upset about this. That, for once, he'd been made the fool.

"You were pretty bad." Estrid sounded way too cheerful.

"It wasn't your fault." I waved a hand at Estrid as if shooing her. "You heard Ravyn. Savarah is an empath. She had influence over us."

Erik furrowed his brow at me. "You're forgetting something."

"What?"

"We're D'ahvol," Estrid chimed in.

"Magic does not affect us. Anything I did was, sadly, of my own volition." Erik's cheeks were red, and I didn't think it was from the fresh air.

"I don't know," I said slowly, eyes on the ground as I thought about it. Every time Savarah was around, I felt different. Agitated. "Maybe it's different with her. We're immune to magic, not to charm."

We'd reentered the part of the forest with the massive trees. The temple tree loomed in front of us, and now that I knew what I was looking for, was impossible to miss. Larger and more elegant than its neighbors, the bark was scrawled with runes and unfamiliar designs. Ravyn pushed open the backdoor and disappeared inside with Eoghan and Arun.

"Either way," I continued, "I forgive you. If you forgive me."

It was Erik's turn to ask, "For what?"

"For everything. For the life-debt. For taking the job from Tsarra Trisfina. For presuming to free you from your debt by dueling with Luthair."

Erik pressed his lips together and huffed through his nose. "Oh, Frida."

But I didn't get to find out what he was going to say, because the ground trembled. The force of the quake shook the temple tree and knocked the three of us off our feet. I went sprawling over a root. Pain shot through my already injured shoulder and I grimaced.

As I was pushing myself back up, Ravyn emerged from the door, her eyes wild with fear.

"What was it?" Estrid was already running toward her. "A quake?"

But Ravyn was waving her arms, motioning for us to go back. "We're under attack!" she finally managed to say.

I collapsed back down to the ground and groaned. There was no doubt in my mind that the ur'gels had found us. They'd likely seen the ship in the treetops, visible to anything flying overhead. And they were hunting me because Savarah knew about the mark and what Beru believed. Another battle, more death, and it was all my fault.

But I didn't get a chance to wallow in my pity. Erik stepped up beside me and lifted me to my feet by the back of my vest.

"Come on," he said. "We have another fight to win."

# CHAPTER 17

Ravyn had horses and trees fighting on her side, but the ur'gels had—

"What is that?" I asked aghast from my spot on the ground beside Ravyn.

The priest rubbed a hand down her face and sank back into the undergrowth. "That is an armored tusker."

We'd crawled around the side of the tree to get a look at our attackers. The ur'gels were familiar—deformed, humanoid creatures, some of them uglier than others. But this time, several of them were on the back of an enormous, four-legged animal. Its skin was wrinkled and leathery except for its head and long trunk-like nose, which were covered in armored plates. Two giant tusks angled downward, out of its mouth, perfect for spearing us.

"How dangerous is it?" Erik asked.

Ravyn considered. "Alone, it's only dangerous if you get in its way. I'd say that right now, the greatest danger lies in the fact that it is under the control of what I assume are ur'gels, who will use that size against us."

I immediately saw the reason in her logic. The ur'gels had

brought the armored tusker for a reason, and it wouldn't be to kill us. There were easier ways to do that. "They're going to destroy the temple."

No sooner had the words left my mouth than the ur'gels began to drive the tusker forward. The closer it got, the larger I realized it was. Instead of crashing into the tree that contained the temple, it just pushed its armored head against the trunk. Its gigantic, round feet dug grooves through the undergrowth, ripping bushes and smaller trees right out of the ground. Behind it, dozens of ur'gels held onto ropes attached to the beast's neck and whipped its back legs.

The three of us scrambled back, away from the monster and the tree that was cracking and groaning beneath the assault. Estrid was inside, evacuating the other residents of the temple. Eoghan had taken Arun and fled back into the forest, where Ravyn promised me the trees would keep him safe. So it was just the three of us against a dozen ur'gels and a giant armored tusker.

"Who has a plan?" I asked, glad we were small enough to go unnoticed.

Erik wasn't paying attention, though. His head was tilted back, and he was staring at the ur'gels on the tusker's back.

"What is it?"

"Is that—" he started, but was cut off by a shout from the tusker's back.

"Harder, you stupid beast!" It was a familiar female voice, and the sound of it raised the hairs on the back of my neck.

I stumbled back a few steps and shielded my eyes with my hand to get a better view.

Sure enough, there she was, Dag'draath's most loyal subject and the bane of my existence these last few days. Savarah rode astride the tusker, right behind its shoulder blades. In her hands were leather reins. The other end of the reins wrapped around the base of the animal's pointed tusks. There was an exceptionally large ur'gel with her, too, one of the winged ones. He sat beside her, one meaty hand on her shoulder. They looked like old friends. It was obvious they were the ones in charge here.

Any thought I'd had of careful strategizing disappeared. I ran forward, slipping on leaves and debris, until I reached the tusker's foot. I launched myself forward, grabbing the tough, wrinkled skin and climbing.

"Frida!" Erik was not far behind me, but I couldn't let him talk me out of this.

When I was several meters off the ground, the tusker slipped and went down to one knee, very nearly knocking me off. But I held on, my feet scrambling for purchase against the slick skin. I wished for Stiarna, who always had a way of appearing when I needed her the most. But we'd left her back at the ship recovering from her fight with the horses. She had no way of knowing where we even were.

Before I could reach the creature's back, there came an inhuman shout of alarm from the ground. I looked down and saw I'd been spotted. Several ur'gels were sounding the alarm, pointing at me with their long-handled whips, abandoning their posts and beginning to climb. When the ur'gel with Savarah peered over the edge, I pressed myself flat against the tusker. He shouted something incoherent at the ur'gels and turned away, drawing shouts of protest from below.

Erik and Ravyn wasted no time silencing them. Ravyn's blade flashed with light as she cut down the dark creatures with cool, calm precision. Erik, on the other hand, seemed to be unleashing his anger and frustration on the ur'gels. Even as I kept climbing, I could hear his grunts and growls as he brutally destroyed the monsters with his Ahvoli blade.

I had nearly reached the top when someone grabbed the back of my shirt and hauled me up, dangling me precariously over the edge of the monster. My eyes met two dark orbs set in a twisted, leathery face. Two fang-like incisors protruded over the ur'gel's bottom lip and he made a horrible sucking sound between them before he spoke in a gravelly voice.

"Look what we have here. The prize came to us instead." Then, twisting around to Savarah, "I thought you said she would be difficult to catch."

Savarah passed the animal's reins off to another ur'gel and stepped toward me. She was sure-footed, even as the tusker's back swayed beneath us. "Don't let your guard down too easily, my dear." One of her smooth, pale hands caressed my cheek. If I hadn't been holding onto the ur'gel's wrist to keep from falling, I would have swatted her away. "She's tricky. After all, she is descended from Onen Suun."

"No," I grunted out through gritted teeth, tightening my grip on the ur'gel's arm. "I'm. Not."

I swung my legs up and connected solidly with the ur'gel's chest. He fell back and took me with him so I landed on top of him. His hand was still wrapped in my collar and he pulled me close. His breath was hot and smelled like a stable that desperately needed mucking. I gagged and dug my fingers into his eyes, not letting go even as black blood seeped out and pooled around my thumbs.

Finally, he released my shirt and threw me off him. I skidded to a stop at the very rear of the tusker's back, grabbing the base of the tail to stop my slide.

The ur'gel was back on his feet, wiping his eyes and snarling at me. Savarah was hiding behind him and had even put a few other ur'gels between us. She obviously preferred sparring with words to fighting with fists.

I drew my sword and ax and did my best to assume a fighting stance, though it was difficult when the surface below me was rocking and swaying. The ur'gel laughed, his smile revealing rotten, black teeth, and pulled his own weapon. It was a heavy spiked ball at the end of a thick chain. It had to weigh a ton, but he held it as easily as I did my ax.

Beyond him, Savarah cracked the reins. The temple tree groaned and cracked but held as the tusker continued to drive forward. I didn't know why she didn't stop if I was who they'd come for. Maybe I wasn't enough. Maybe it would never be enough for them until they'd destroyed everything good in this world. That meant we were on the cusp of another Dark War, and we had to find the one who could put an end to it, because it definitely wasn't me.

The ur'gel took a step forward, swinging the ball and chain lazily overhead. I took a step back, my foot nearly slipping off the tusker. But I caught myself, shuffled forward, and swung the sword. The ur'gel brought his weapon around and they crashed together. The chain wrapped around the blade and jerked it out of my hand, sending the sword tumbling to the ground.

I watched it fall. "Well, that doesn't seem fair."

The ur'gel didn't laugh this time. He swung the chain again and I danced to the side. When the spiked ball hit the tusker's back, I thought I heard the beast cry in protest, but it was hard to tell over the other sounds from the fight below.

I spun away from the ur'gel and brought my ax around with me. Using my momentum, I buried the ax in the ur'gel's blue-skinned chest.

He looked down at it, then back up at me, his mouth cracked open in shock. Then, he wrapped his clawed fingers around the handle just above where my hands still gripped it and jerked it out with a growl. Blood streamed from the wound, leaving black streaks down his stomach.

"Stupid human," he grumbled, looking up at me.

"I'm not—"

But I didn't get a chance to finish. His big, meaty hand came across my face and sent me spinning sideways and off the back of the tusker.

"No!" I heard Savarah shout.

I twisted and managed to grab the tusker's thin tail with one hand, swinging to a stop a few yards above the battle on the ground. Other priests had emerged from the temple and joined the fight against the ur'gels, as had a few more trehands. One of them reached a branch up and plucked me from where I hung, wooden fingers wrapping around my waist and lowering me to the ground beside Ravyn, who stood behind it.

She looked sideways at me, and down at the ax dripping black blood. Her own blade was coated in the same substance, and when she brushed her long, dark hair back from her face, she left a streak of it across her cheek. "We have to stop the tusker."

The ur'gels on the tusker's back were still driving it forward. The temple tree was leaning perilously, its branches trembling under the strain.

I pressed a hand to my throbbing face. "How?"

Savarah's voice was the one that answered. She was leaning over the back of the tusker. "Surrender yourself and I'll spare your temple."

I didn't believe her. "What else do you have?" I asked Ravyn.

She motioned me forward and I followed, running alongside the tusker's legs and toward the tree. We passed Erik, who speared an ur'gel on the end of his sword, and Estrid, protecting his back from an onslaught of smaller, winged ur'gels. When Ravyn beckoned them, they came after us.

As we neared the front, we ducked to the side to avoid the grooves the tusker had dug in the earth and stood in a half ring, shoulder-to-shoulder at the base of the tree. We were close to the tusker, but it didn't pay us any attention, as small as we were. Its head pressed against the tree, and its long, armored trunk hung just in front of us. Behind us, the tree trunk began to splinter.

An ur'gel ran at us, and I sliced through its neck with one swing of the ax. It fell at our feet.

I wiped the ax on the grass. "What now?"

"Protect me." Ravyn sheathed her sword and held her hands out in front of her. "Whatever you do, don't let them get through to me."

"Wait, what?"

But she was already gone. That was the only way to describe it. Her hands were on the curve of the tusker's trunk, but her eyes were somewhere else. As if she had become someone—or something—else.

Just as I thought it, the tusker stopped its assault on the temple. It jerked backward, rearing briefly on two feet and landing with a thud. Several ur'gels toppled from its back not far from us. Before my siblings could run forward to dispatch them, the tusker lifted one of its massive front feet and brought it down on top of the fallen ur'gels, crushing them. The beast reared again and more ur'gels fell, screaming.

I watched for a flash of golden curls, waited for Savarah to fall, but she never appeared. The ones that did fall were squashed beneath the tusker's feet or swept away with its trunk. The tusker was noticeably careful not to knock over any trees but had absolutely no consideration for the ur'gels. It scooped up one in its trunk and bashed it against the ground until it hung limp, then flung it aside.

It was terrifying to watch, and obviously unnatural. Ravyn herself had told me tuskers weren't inherently dangerous or violent, but this either proved her wrong, or proved the extent of her magic.

This was all it took for the ur'gels who were left standing to flee. They left the bodies of their comrades broken and bloody on the forest floor and disappeared into the foliage.

"Where's Savarah?" I asked no one in particular. "Did anyone see her?"

Erik pointed up and I watched as the winged ur'gel I had wounded leapt from the tusker's back, Savarah in his arms. While the tusker was occupied with another group of ur'gels, this one swooped down to hover a few yards above us. I wished for Arun and his bow then, but he was squirreled away somewhere with Eoghan, hopefully recovering.

"This isn't the end of this," Savarah shouted down to me. "I'll be back. Dag'draath will be very interested to know of your existence."

"Dag'draath is locked away in an eternal prison," I countered.

"He will be freed. And if you won't help me free him, then I'll make sure you can't help keep him imprisoned either."

The tusker turned on her then, but the ur'gel was too fast for its swinging trunk. It followed them from the ground, though, crashing through the undergrowth. When it had disappeared from sight, Ravyn collapsed against me, her work done, her temple safe.

But as the other priests collected her and we followed her inside, I couldn't help but feel disappointed Savarah had, once again, gotten away. This wasn't fun anymore, and it was time to get some answers.

# CHAPTER 18

Ravyn slept the rest of the day, and I kept watch by her bedside. I told myself it was because I needed to talk to her, and not because Arun occupied the next bed over. He also slept, both of them still as corpses. Every now and then, I'd put my hand on Arun's chest to be sure he was still breathing. He was, and the amulet was gone from around his neck. Destroyed, I hoped, along with the darkness inside of him.

The room had grown dark when Erik entered, carrying a steaming bowl. "Dinner?"

I shrugged, taking the bowl from him. It contained a thin broth with chunks of vegetables floating in it. I sipped it, watching him go from bed to bed.

"How are they?"

"Alive," I answered.

He sat on a small, wooden stool and crossed his arms over his broad chest. "Can you believe what happened today?"

"Which part?" I sipped steadily at the soup. I hadn't realized just how hungry I'd been. Fighting had a way of working up my appetite.

"All of it, I guess."

If there was anything I knew about my brother, it was he did not like the unknown. He did not like *not* knowing something. So, I could see how this place and everything that had happened since our arrival had been a nightmare for him.

I pushed myself to my feet and deposited the empty bowl on a table beside Arun's bed. "I've gotten pretty good at believing the unbelievable lately."

Not long after Erik left, leaving me a torchlight to hang by the door, Arun stirred. He looked pale and gaunt in the light of the fire, but when he opened his eyes, they were no longer black orbs. It was a relief to look into his green eyes again, to see the spark of life behind them.

His voice was hoarse when he finally spoke. "What happened?"

I passed him a glass of water. "What's the last thing you remember?"

He thought about it as he sipped at the drink. "Sitting down to dinner. We were … inside a tree."

"Still are." I gestured to the room around us, and then sat on the edge of his bed. "You attacked me at dinner. The priest threw you into the Lake of Light to cure you. While you slept it off, we beat back an ur'gel attack. And now, here we are."

"Never a dull moment with you around, is there?" He shook his head. Then his hand went to his throat.

"It's gone," I told him. "The amulet."

"What happened to it?"

"I don't know. But you seem to be doing okay without it."

His hand fumbled for something in the bed and then closed around my fingers. The relief at feeling his warm skin again was enough to make me not pull away.

"Do you feel different?" I asked, wondering how the Lake of Light might have changed him. If it had burned out any part of what made him who he was.

He closed his eyes and his voice was quieter when he said, "I feel lighter."

He drifted back to sleep, his hand still wrapped around mine.

I must have dozed off also, my head on the edge of Arun's bed, because I jerked awake some time later to the light of the white moon shining through the window. It lit Ravyn's pale face and showed me her eyes were open.

I moved away from Arun and went to stand beside her. "How do you feel?"

"Fine." She flexed her fingers and studied them in the moonlight. "Sometimes I worry that I won't come back."

"So, it was you, then, inside the tusker?" I'd thought as much, but it was a strange concept to grasp.

"Yes, it was." She pushed herself to sitting and flung the blanket off her legs.

I sat down on the edge of her bed before she could stand. "We need to talk."

She paused, looking at me warily. Her eyes flicked to Arun on the other bed. "How is he?"

"Not about him," I countered. "But he seems to be fine, thanks to you."

"Thanks to the light," she corrected me.

I shifted on the bed and then caught her eyes with mine. "Ravyn, I need to know what's going on. I need to know what you know about me, and about this." I touched the star on the side of my face.

Ravyn sighed, clearly having expected this line of questioning. "I'll tell you what I can. First thing's first: I know for a certainty that you are *not* the Suun heir."

It took every ounce of my self-control not to jump for joy there in the middle of the infirmary. I'd known it, of course, but finally having someone confirm it? Well, maybe now things could get back to normal.

There was still more, though. "Why do I have his mark, then?"

"When Onen Suun made the great sacrifice that ended the Dark War and imprisoned Dag'draath, a priest received a prophecy that has been passed down through the order of the Sisters of Light over the generations."

"So, you are the Sisters of Light, then? As Lunla told us?"

Ravyn nodded, and then continued. "It was foretold that the Suun line would continue, and that there would be born an heir with the mark of Suun. This heir would bring an end to Dag'-draath's imprisonment and would usher forth the next era of the fight between the light and the dark."

"That wasn't what Beru said." On the contrary, he seemed to think the Suun heir would be the one to stop the war.

She held up a finger before I could go too far down that path, though. "But the heir would also have the power to keep Dag'draath in his prison."

"So, she has a choice."

Ravyn smiled secretly. "There's always a choice, isn't there?"

"Who is the heir, then? Why aren't they here, fighting this fight? Why has it fallen to me?"

"She was born two decades ago, just after I'd been inducted into the Sisters of Light. The mother brought the babe to us in a panic. I cannot describe to you what it was like to look down on that child and know I was looking into the eyes of the Suun heir. Of the one who would either bring us into the light or doom us to eternal darkness." Ravyn touched the mark beside my eye, her fingers cold as ice. "That was how I knew, from the moment I first saw you, that you were not that same babe."

"What became of her?" I needed to find her if I wanted to prove to everyone I was not the heir.

Ravyn put both of her feet on the floor and stared straight ahead at where Arun lay, but I did not think she was seeing him. "She lived with us for a time, but we quickly learned that it would be too dangerous for her to carry both the mark and the burden of being the heir. She would always be a target for those wishing to thwart the prophecy. So my sisters devised a plan.

"There was another child born on the same day in a faraway corner of the world. A child of warriors, who would grow up to become one herself. We would transfer the mark onto this child and leave her to make her own way in the world. Every day would be a fight for survival, but who was more equipped for that life than a D'ahvol?"

I stood and grabbed my stomach, suddenly afraid that I would be sick.

Ravyn put a hand on my arm so I couldn't run away. "You wanted the truth. I will give it to you. But sometimes the truth is worse than the lie."

"What happened to my mother?"

"It should have been an easy task, to sneak in and perform the transfer and leave without anyone ever knowing. But you made a sound, barely louder than a bird's chirp. Your mother woke."

I shook Ravyn's hand off my arm and pressed my back was against the rough wood of a wall. I sank down on my haunches, refusing to look at the priest as she kept talking.

In my mind's eye, I was back at our home in Bor'sur. My mother would have fallen asleep beside the hearth, with me bundled in furs at her side, lulled by the crackling flames. Father would have been in his room, while Erik and Estrid slept in the loft overhead. I could hear the tinkle of snow on the roof, the whistle of wind through the eaves. And there, the crunch of snow beneath a foot. The creak of an opening door. Hands lifting me from the cradle, spiriting me outside. My mother waking, finding me outside with the priest.

"Your mother fought bravely, but she was no match for the light."

"For a sword, you mean." I wrapped my arms around myself,

my mind reeling. "Not only did you mark me as a target for all the evil in the world, but you left me without a mother to guide me through it."

"We could not be discovered. It was to protect the heir."

"And what about me? I'm just the bait?"

"More like the distraction."

I scoffed. "You don't see anything wrong with this?"

She pressed her lips together and for the first time, I thought maybe I saw doubt on her features. "It was a choice we had to make, and every choice has consequences. None of them are easy."

I pushed myself to standing, grief giving way to anger. "You won't tell me where she is, will you?"

Ravyn stood too, smoothing down her smock dress. "I can't, because I don't know. After the transfer, she was taken away and put under the protection of four of my sisters. Only they know where she is." She started toward the door.

I took a few steps forward, stopping beside Arun's bed and watching her leave. "For now," I said.

She stopped and glanced back at me. "What?"

"Only they know where she is *for now*. But you can be sure that I will find her. Your sisters made a big mistake, putting my whole family at risk. I will find her, and I will expose her."

The priest smiled. Even without her sword, it was a frightening look. "If I thought there was any chance you could actually do that, I would kill you now."

But I wasn't afraid. I smiled back at her. "You could try."

They'd picked me because I was a warrior, but they hadn't counted on what that meant when I learned the truth. They hadn't counted on the lengths I would go to, to protect the loved ones I had left.

Ravyn left without another word, the only sounds in the room my heavy breathing as I fought back angry tears. Fingers wrapped around mine and squeezed, drawing me out of my panic.

Surprised, I looked down to see Arun watching me. "Heard that, did you?"

"A bit."

I took my place beside him again. "What do I do now?"

"The way I see it," he said, "they saved the heir so that when the time came, she could save us all. We just have to convince Ravyn that this is that time. That we need her, not because we want to throw her to Dag'draath, but because we want to fulfill the prophecy."

"I might have ruined any chance we have at that already."

Arun laughed, and it was a delightful sound I hadn't realized I was missing until now. "I heard. Maybe let me do the talking next time."

"I don't know if I can agree to that."

He smirked, and then tugged on my hand. "Come here."

When he drew me down beside him on the bed, I surprised myself by not fighting it. Instead, I lay on my side facing away from him and he wrapped an arm over me, pulling me close and curling around me. It felt … nice. More vulnerable than I would have liked, but still nice.

His voice was a low whisper in my ear. "I'm sorry about your mother, and I'm sorry you had to find out this way."

It was easier to talk without looking at him, so I kept my face turned away and willed the tears not to fall. "I always thought she was out there somewhere. That I would see her again. But now I can't decide if it was better not to know. If it's relief or sadness I feel at knowing I can stop looking for her in every crowd we encounter."

"I still look for Ashryn."

His sister, I remembered, the one who'd died. "Do you ever see her?"

He was quiet for a moment before answering. "Everywhere. Bits and pieces of her in everyone."

We fell silent then, and I focused on the feel of his chest rising and falling against my back, on his breath tickling my ear. Eventually, the torchlight flickered out, but neither of us moved until finally, we both fell asleep. For the first time in a long time, I slept through the night.

# CHAPTER 19

When I woke the next morning, I was alone in the infirmary bed. Arun's side of the bed was cold, and I had a brief moment of panic wondering if any of it had been real. Then the door open and Arun strode in, looking good as new.

"Good morning," he said, kicking the door closed behind him. He had a bundle of clothes in his arms. "The priests thought you might like a change of clothes."

I looked down at myself, still speckled with black ur'gel blood. A bath would have been nice, but a change of clothes would do for now. I held up one of the items he dropped on the foot of the bed. "This is a skirt."

He looked over at it. "A dress, actually."

"I don't wear skirts. Or dresses." They were not suitable for fighting. Or running. Or doing much of anything.

"It might look nice."

Even more reason not to wear it. I didn't need him thinking I looked nice, not after last night. Actually, I didn't know why I cared what he thought at all. I shouldn't. I definitely shouldn't.

But I did.

No, I didn't.

In the light of morning, everything seemed a lot more complicated. I could scarcely believe I had let him hold me and comfort me last night. That he had seen me like that.

Onen save me.

"Get out," I ordered, not wanting to think about it—him—anymore. "So I can change."

He left, and I dressed quickly. The skirt left my legs feeling bare and strange. I knew that in many parts of the world, women were practically forbidden to wear trousers, but the Western March was not one of them. In fact, women were more likely to carry an ax or a sword in Bor'sur than wear a skirt. My boots, at least, provided some protection to my feet and lower legs.

When I opened the door, Arun was leaning against the wall, picking under his nails with a small knife. He looked up and smiled, genuinely happy to see me. It stopped me in my tracks. Was he there just as a friendly gesture? Or was it something more? Something I'd brought on by my behavior last night.

"I have it on good authority that Ravyn is out hunting this morning," he said, tucking his knife away inside his vest. "I thought we could help her."

"Why?" I asked cautiously.

"Well, helping Lunla got us this far, maybe helping Ravyn can convince her of our good intentions."

To be frank, I didn't know that my intentions *were* all that good. I would do whatever it took to keep my family safe and to be able to return home. Even if that meant sacrificing the heir, who'd been so willing to sacrifice me and my mother all those years ago.

But I didn't have a problem lying to get what I wanted. "Sure."

I wasn't much of a hunter, but Arun seemed excited, grabbing his bow and a quiver of arrows on our way out of the temple. With everything super-sized in this part of the forest, I couldn't imagine what we were hunting. How big were rabbits and wild boar in these parts, anyway? Did I really want to find out? I guessed I did if I wanted to eat something other than vegetable stew.

Arun paused outside the temple, looked around, and then headed south. The veil was thick, casting the forest in eerie shadows. There was no sound except for the crunching of the leaves under our feet.

A gentle gust of wind ruffled my skirts and I pushed them down with my hands, regretting the decision to surrender my pants. "How did you know to come this way?"

"The wind," Arun answered. "She wouldn't want to be upwind from her prey."

Great, so we'd be going into the wind the whole time. I just hoped I wouldn't give Arun a show if the wind picked up.

After walking for just a few more minutes, Arun knelt and brushed his fingers on the base of a tree where the bark had scraped away. "Boar." Then he touched a section of leaves that had been pressed down by a heavy boot. "Priest."

We followed the trail until we came to an oversized oak tree on the bank of a small, winding creek and Arun pulled me down beside it. Without speaking, he pointed across the creek to a small clearing. It took me a minute to find her, but I eventually spotted Ravyn squatting behind a bush, her bow raised and an arrow ready to fly. Across from her was a wild boar rooting through the undergrowth.

Ravyn shifted and when she did, a branch cracked loud enough we heard it from where we were across the creek. The boar looked up, white tusks glinting as it turned its gaze on her. Ravyn released her arrow.

Arun gave a sharp intake of breath as the priest's arrow whizzed past the animal and it charged right for her. He stood, nocked his own arrow, and released it, barely taking the time to aim. The boar squealed, took two more steps, and collapsed at Ravyn's feet, an arrow protruding from just above its shoulder.

The priest turned around and saw us there. She gave a small nod before kneeling beside the body.

I followed Arun, splashing through the creek. "You're pretty good at saving these priests' lives."

He chuckled. "Right place, right time, I guess." Then he handed me his bow and approached Ravyn. "How can we help?"

She looked at him over her shoulder before turning back to the boar. "You already have. I don't know why you're here, but I'm glad for it."

Blood gurgled out of the wound and soaked the boar's shiny black coat. She used a knife to make holes in the back legs and then the three of us hoisted the body up on a rope so that it hung from a tree. Then Ravyn made a long cut from the head to the tail and began skinning the boar.

"I was not sure you would still be here … after last night."

This, I knew, was directed at me. "Why would I leave when you have what I want?"

Arun shot me a warning glance behind Ravyn's back.

She peeled off another strip of skin and discarded it. Her hands were stained red with blood. "I already told you, I don't know where the heir is."

Arun sidled up to her and took his own knife to the boar's skin. "But I'm guessing you know how to find her."

I stood back, my arms crossed over my chest.

"Even if I could—"

"You wouldn't, I know." Arun sheathed his knife and held a hand out to me.

Rolling my eyes, I pulled my ax from my belt and handed it to him. He made a cut to the back of the boar's neck and then began to saw through the spine to remove the head. Once it was off, the corpse would be light enough to carry back to the temple.

But we didn't get that far. Before he could finish removing the head, another priest burst out of the forest and splashed across the creek.

"Thank Onen I found you." She leaned against a tree, panting. She was older, her dark hair streaked with grey.

Ravyn had already gone to her and taken her hands. "What is it?"

"The ur'gels. They're back."

I snatched my ax from Arun. "Where are they?" But the forest around us was still silent.

"No, they haven't attacked yet. They've gathered in the valley. They're coming. We have to leave."

"Leave?" Ravyn drew back from the other priest.

Looking at the shock on her face, I realized what I could do for her in exchange for the information I needed. We didn't need to help her. We needed to save her temple.

I turned to her, ignoring Arun's warning looks. The ur'gels weren't here because they cared about Ravyn or the temple. They wanted me because they thought I was the Suun heir. "I can draw them away. But I won't leave until I know where to find the heir. She's been hiding long enough. If she's supposed to save the world, this is the time."

Ravyn hesitated, and I could see how it was tearing her apart. She wanted to protect her temple, but also the Suun heir. "What choice do I really have?"

I remembered her own words from earlier. "There's always a choice."

"Will you help her? Can you promise me that?"

My first instinct was to say no. I didn't know if I could promise that. But then I caught Arun's eye over her shoulder. If ever there was a lost cause, this was it. I'd been afraid to step into the Lake of Light because of the darkness inside of me. Maybe this was my chance to redeem myself. "Yes. We will help her."

Ravyn turned to the other priest. "We'll require your assistance."

She seemed to know exactly what it was that Ravyn was asking of her. "Of course. This way."

We followed her back toward the temple but veered off the path onto a small, hidden game trail.

"Where are we going?" I asked Ravyn.

"The scrying pool. Typhna is a seer."

"A seer?" Arun sounded impressed.

I was less so. "We're supposed to trust a seer?"

"It's that or go on information that's almost twenty years old. Take your pick."

The scrying pool was really just a basin of water contained in the sawed-off trunk of a tree at waist level. It seemed more like a puddle than a magical pool, but knowing how they loved their trees, I kept my mouth shut.

The other priest, Typhna, stood before the tree, her hands hovering over the still water within. The rest of us gathered around and stared into the pool. All I saw was my reflection looking back at me.

"We're looking for the Sisters of Light who are guarding the Suun heir," Ravyn explained to Typhna.

Typhna nodded and stared intently at the water.

"What does she see?" Arun whispered to Ravyn.

"It depends on what we ask of her. Sometimes she can see over great distances, sometimes she can see the future. Sometimes, she sees nothing at all."

"Doesn't sound that impressive to me," I scoffed. I couldn't believe I was going to go chasing down a girl based on a maybe-vision from a second-rate seer.

Arun rolled his eyes at me.

Ravyn, though, smiled at me. "You'll see."

Finally, Typhna, who'd been quiet this whole time, touched

one finger to the center of the pool. The touch rippled out in circular rings, and my reflection began to change.

I held my breath and watched, trying to decide if it was a trick of my eyes as my face became someone else's, though the star beside my eye remained. My skin and hair grew darker, and my features morphed into those of a beautiful girl with a round face and delicate features.

But when I blinked, she was gone, and in her place was an old woman's body lying prone on the forest floor. She wore the orange robes of a priest, and her grey hair was in a cloud around her head. Her dull, grey eyes were open, and I realized they were reflecting the ever-present veil of clouds that hung over Bruhier.

Typhna touched the water again, and as quickly as she'd come, the woman was gone.

# CHAPTER 20

"What?" I looked at each face gathered around the scrying pool. Arun looked just as confused as I did. Typhna looked slightly apologetic. And Ravyn looked grave, her mouth drawn down in a frown. "Who was that? *Where* was that?"

"That was one of my sisters," Ravyn answered, her eyes still on the water.

"Is she dead now? Or was that a future vision?"

Typhna bit her lip. "It's hard to say, but I believe the woman's death is yet to come."

I opened my mouth to yell at her, but Arun's hand came down on my shoulder and I kept my frustration to myself. It was a good thing, too, I realized. She had to be frustrated too, being able to see someone's future and not being able to do anything about it.

Ravyn stooped and picked up a rock from the ground. She held it in one fist for a moment, her eyes closed. Then, she held it out to me across the scrying pool. "Here."

I took it by reflex. "What do you want me to do with this?"

"In your hands, and only your hands, it will guide you to the Suun heir."

I turned it over in my hand. It was a grey rock, smooth and round and completely normal.

"Remember your promise to me. Help her. You must get to her before the ur'gels do." She came around the pool and closed my hand around the rock. "They will kill her, unless you can stop them. Her life is in your hands. It always has been."

"But what will the rock do?"

"You and the heir are forever linked. The rock has been enchanted to give you the guidance you need to find your way back to her."

We made our way back to the temple, Ravyn and Typhna walking ahead of Arun and me.

I took the opportunity to ask Arun what he thought about the vision in the pool. "Who do you think that first girl was?"

"What first girl?"

My skirt got caught on a branch and I jerked it free. I couldn't wait to get out of this thing. "The one who appeared in the pool before the old woman."

His brows drew together. "There was no one before the old woman."

He seemed to certain about it that I dropped the subject.

Frida and Erik met us outside the temple, already wearing their clean clothes and armor, weapons in their hands.

"The ur'gels are coming," Erik announced.

"We know." I held up the rock as if it would offer some kind of explanation. "We're leaving. We'll draw them away."

"Is that really a good idea?" Estrid asked. Then, she looked me up and down. "Why are you wearing a skirt?"

I rolled my eyes at her, foregoing a response.

We ducked inside the temple where we were met by Eoghan. The tree offered me my clean, folded clothes, which I took gratefully.

Arun turned off toward the kitchen. "I'll get supplies. You get changed. Meet me out front."

It was with great relief I donned my pants, tunic, and leather armor. I strapped on my weapons belts, Estrid handing me my ax and sword as we ran for the door.

I filled her in as we went.

"A seer and a magic stone?" Estrid looked as dubious as I felt.

"We've seen stranger things," I said with a shrug.

Back outside, things still seemed normal. Arun and Erik had bags of supplies slung over their shoulders.

Arun shrugged me off when I offered to take one. "Do you have the stone?" he asked.

I pulled it from an inner pocket of my vest and showed it to him.

"Your only job is to make sure you and that stone make it onto the ship."

Ravyn rounded the tree then on the back of her horse-beast. To my surprise, a handful of other priests followed her, also mounted. The horses pranced restlessly as they drew near us.

Estrid grunted and took a step back. "One man's monster is another man's pet, I suppose."

"I'm not so sure those horses are anyone's pets."

As if to prove my point, Ravyn's horse snorted, sending a plume of smoke into the sky. Ravyn wheeled him around. "We'll take you to the ship and make sure you get on board. The rest is up to you."

Eoghan was there too, the only trehand present, but I felt eyes on us from all around and wondered how many were watching us from their places in the forest. He led the way, weaving in and out of the trees skillfully. Ravyn and her priests brought up the rear.

I was right behind Eoghan, so when an ur'gel bounded out of the trees and leapt on his back, I was on him in just a few seconds. The ur'gel had his black claws dug deep under the bark of what seemed to be Eoghan's shoulders. The trehand thrashed wildly, reaching his branches over his head and behind him to try to shake the ur'gel off.

It wasn't working. I heard Ravyn galloping up behind us, but I didn't know if she would make it on time or what she could even do against the monster. Instead, I drew my ax, pulled it back over my shoulder, and let it fly without missing a step. There was always the risk I would hit Eoghan, but I trusted myself in this, at least. I'd been throwing axes for practically as long as I'd been holding one.

The ax hit the ur'gel square between the shoulder blades and he fell into a screaming pile on the ground. Estrid was there first, driving her sword into the monster's neck. I stopped to scoop up the ax and we kept running.

But more ur'gels were coming out of hiding. I dropped two with my ax but three more emerged from the shadows, all of them converging on me. I was fighting them off when something sharp grabbed my shoulders and lifted me off the ground. In my shock, I dropped my ax and could only watch as one of the horrible, blue-skinned beasts picked it up and laughed.

It was impossible to say what else was happening around us. The pain in my shoulder was intense and all-consuming. My fingers pried at the claws there as I tried to extricate myself from their grasp. I ground my teeth together and tried not to scream as the ur'gel lifted me higher and higher into the air.

A hand around my ankle stopped our climb and tugged me back down until my feet touched the ground. There was a grunt, and a thud, and I was free, falling into a heap on the forest floor. Blood trickled out of the small puncture wounds in my shoulders, but it wasn't as bad as when the ur'gel had speared me in Barepost. When I looked up, Arun was standing over me, my ax in his hand and the supplies still slung over his shoulder.

"I believe this belongs to you." He offered it to me hilt first.

Standing, I took it from him, wiping the black ur'gel blood on my pants. "Thanks. And you didn't even drop the food."

He smiled and winked, then grabbed my hand and dragged me forward to join the others who had already reached the tree where the ship was docked. Shadebig blood still speckled the ground around it, but the bodies were mostly gone, save for a few random, gruesome body parts still scattered about. I didn't want to think about what had happened to them, what had eaten them or stolen them away.

The ur'gels were also closing in. We could hear them crashing through the underbrush. Ravyn and her priests made a circle around us on their horses.

"Go," Ravyn said. "We'll hold them off."

As if on cue, an ur'gel burst forward, claws reaching for her horse. The horse-beast reared back, baring its fangs, and bit into the ur'gels neck, ripping its head from its body in a spray of black blood.

I turned away from the carnage and took the boost that Arun offered, scrambling for the lowest branch, and pulled myself up. Once I was there, I turned back and offered him my hand. He took it and joined me, then stood and boosted me to the next branch.

Estrid and Erik were already halfway up the tree and urging us on, while below, Ravyn and the priests kept the ur'gels from following us. Thankfully, there did not seem to be any other fliers among them, so we were safe, at least for now.

Stiarna met us as we scaled the ship's side, clucking at us angrily. I scratched behind her ears in an attempt to console her.

At the helm, Arun took the wheel and gently raised the lever. Erik, Estrid, and I unfurled the sails and prepared for takeoff. The *Iron Duchess* groaned and rocked as she freed herself from the treetops and took to the air. I stood at the railing, watching the forest grow smaller as we rose.

The wind caught the sails and carried us away from the trees and back to the south, until we were over the valley where we'd first encountered the horses. It was now where the ur'gels camped. Crude tents had been erected, the largest right beside the river. I watched as the flap opened and a woman stepped out, the sun glinting off of her golden curls. Savarah turned her face skyward and watched the ship sail over her head. Another figure emerged from the tent, this one a winged ur'gel with a bandage over his chest. It had to be the same one I'd fought on the back of the tusker.

He and Savarah conferred and then he launched himself into the air, black, leathery wings flapping powerfully. Arun had left his bow and quiver on the deck, so I snatched up the bow and plucked an arrow from the quiver.

Arun did a double-take when I ran past him with the weapon. "What are you doing?" But from where he stood at the helm, he wouldn't be able to see our pursuer.

I had never been very good at using a bow. I lacked the patience and preferred the personal aspect of hand-to-hand combat. But like every D'ahvol, I'd trained in a variety of weapons and was no stranger to archery. So I nocked the arrow, drew the string back until it touched the corner of my mouth, and aimed at the winged beast who was quickly gaining on us. I took aim, focusing on the white bandage, then below the wound I'd already put there.

The arrow flew straight and true, burying its pointed tip in the creature's chest. He stopped climbing and instead grasped the shaft of the arrow and pulled it from his chest. The wound was pouring black blood. His eyes closed, and he plummeted out of the sky, soon becoming nothing but a black splotch against the green and brown grass of the valley below.

## CHAPTER 21

Just because their leader had fallen did not mean the ur'gels were ready to give up. They were launching rocks and sticks at the bottom of the *Iron Duchess*, who seemed to be struggling to rise above the clouds of the veil.

"We need more wind," Arun said. "The sheriu box can only get us up, not out." He gestured to the blue box at the very top of the mainmast.

It wasn't until he said it I realized how still the air was. I walked to the front of the ship where my siblings stood watching the thick crowd of ur'gels beneath us. A stick sailed over the railing. I picked it up and lobbed it back over, hoping it would at least knock one of them out. A series of large rocks came next. Most of them landed harmlessly on the deck but one flew past me to the other side and cracked Estrid on the back of the head.

My sister toppled forward, the railing catching her at the waist. Her feet went over her head and she was gone from view.

Erik and I both rushed to where she'd been standing, expecting to see her falling to the ground, but instead, she was hanging from the hull nets. The rocks and sticks had stopped coming. Instead, the ur'gels on the ground had gotten loud with excitement, waiting for her to fall so they could tear her to pieces.

I hoisted myself up on the railing. "Don't let go."

"Believe me, I won't." Her voice edged with panic.

I stepped over the railing. Erik took my hand and I dropped down to where Estrid was still hanging. I reached down to her. "Take my hand."

She looked down at the crowd below us. When she did, I saw the blood matting the back of her head, turning her yellow hair red. Then, looking back at me, she said, "I can't."

"What do you mean?" I stretched even further, until she would barely have to reach for me. "Of course, you can."

"I don't feel so good." She squeezed her eyes closed and her fingers slid slightly against the rope as she loosened her grip.

"Lower," I hissed at Erik.

He grimaced and stretched until I could almost touch Estrid's fingers. Stiarna appeared then, swooping over the edge of the ship, and hovering just below Estrid. But Estrid wouldn't accept her help, kicking her feet anytime the griffin got near her.

"Estrid. Estrid. Look at me."

She tore her eyes from the hoard below her dangling toes.

"You will not fall. I cannot lose you. Take my hand."

A breeze caught the ship's sails and we rose suddenly. Estrid gasped and released the net with one hand, clapping it instead around my wrist.

"Pull us in," I ordered Erik.

He heaved us back over the railing and the three of us collapsed in a heap on the deck. As soon as Estrid looked up, I reached out and punched her in the arm. Hard.

"What's wrong with you?" I snapped.

Estrid groaned and rolled to the side, holding her arm where

I'd hit her. She didn't answer. Erik crawled to her and began to examine the cut on the back of her head.

I stalked away toward the helm, Stiarna on my heels. We were still below the veil but high enough the rocks and other projectiles didn't reach us and moving fast enough we were soon out of view of the ur'gels.

Arun glanced at me, then away. "I'm glad she's okay."

"Me, too." I didn't tell him she almost wasn't.

"So, where are we headed? Is it time to follow the rock?"

I touched the pocket in my vest, but didn't draw out the stone Ravyn had given me. "I'm not so sure that's a good idea."

"Isn't that why we left?" he asked.

"I promised Ravyn I would help the heir. Is leading the ur'gels right to her really the best way to handle it?"

Estrid and Erik appeared then, Estrid rubbing the back of her head and looking dazed.

Erik was guiding her by the elbow and came to stand beside us. "Estrid filled me in. I have to say, I thought the same thing. If the whole point is to protect the heir, won't our arrival in her hiding place put her in danger?"

Even though it had been the point I was making, it still irked me she was getting such consideration when I got none. The only thing keeping me from going straight there and throwing the girl to the ur'gels was the fact I'd made a promise to Ravyn.

"But there was also the vision," Arun added.

Erik nodded. "Right, the dead woman."

"It's possible, then, that the ur'gels have already found her, or will find her soon. If that's the case, delaying will only guarantee her death."

They both looked at me. "What do you want to do?" Erik asked.

I ran a finger along the edge of my ax. It needed to be sharpened, but that would have to wait. "We need to split up."

"No," Erik said at the same time Arun said, "I'll go with you."

"I'll go alone," I said. "I'll lure the ur'gels away, and you will go after the Suun heir while I keep them—and Savarah—distracted."

Erik was shaking his head even as I spoke. "That's a terrible idea."

I planted my feet firmly, refusing to be swayed. "It's not, and you know it. It's the only viable idea that keeps the heir safe. Isn't it worth it to save the world?"

Arun studied me. "I don't know. Is it?"

Once again, no one was listening to me. I pressed my lips together and looked away.

"Frida," Arun said in a warning tone. "Talk to us."

But I was done. So, I did what I knew would bother him the most. I turned on my heel and walked away, ducking into the crew's quarters below deck. He was flying the ship, so he couldn't pursue me.

The crew's quarters were a dark, paneled room that would have been large except it was stuffed to bursting with wooden crates, kegs, and a wide table where the crew could take their meals. There were about a dozen cots hanging on the walls, stacked tight on top of each other. I'd spent as little time as possible in here, not liking how it reminded me of being trapped in the mines. I had never eaten down here or slept on any of them.

I sat on one now. It rocked gently with the swaying of the ship. I must have drifted off to sleep because the next thing I knew, Estrid was shaking me awake. I didn't know how much time had passed, but she looked better. Alert.

"Erik told me what you said. About leaving."

I blinked up at her, and then pushed myself to sitting. "Yeah."

"I think you're forgetting how important you are to this plan."

The hammock creaked as I turned to look at her. "What do you mean?"

She tucked her hair behind her ear and looked down at her lap. "We can't find the heir without you."

I grunted in acknowledgment. That much was true, if the stone even worked, but we could find a way around it. I could set them on the right path and then make my own way somewhere else, in the opposite direction.

Estrid cleared her throat. "But even if we could... We wouldn't. You know that, right?"

"Why not?" I asked. "If it would save the world? I find it hard to believe that anyone, Erik especially, wouldn't find honor in that."

She laughed. "I'm not talking about honor. I'm talking about family. Even if you'd been the Suun heir, you still would have been a Svand. And Svands don't leave each other." When I didn't respond, she added, "What was it that you said to me earlier? 'I cannot lose you.' Well, little sister, I won't lose you either."

She was right. We had never left Erik. Not when we'd thought he was dead after the shipwreck. Not when he insisted on staying in Barepost to repay his life-debt. We hadn't let Estrid go when she'd nearly fallen off the *Duchess*. But somehow, I'd never thought it was a rule that applied to me.

I couldn't help the small smile that tugged at my lips. "It would be easier if you would just let me go."

"Who needs easy when I have you?" She bumped her shoulder against mine, and then stood. "Now, let's go up there and figure out where we're going so Arun can stop flying us around in circles."

The sun was a low orange ball by the time we emerged, painting the veil in pinks and yellows. We were flying between two towering plateaus whose tops disappeared into the clouds. I peeked over the railing to confirm there were no ur'gels anywhere in sight.

Arun was just where I'd left him, his hands on the ship's wheel. "Feeling better?"

"Yes. I'm—"

He held up a hand to stop me. "We all have our moments. I mean, I attacked you, right? So, it could be worse."

I laughed, despite myself.

"So where to, then? I assume I'm not dropping you off as ur'gel bait somewhere."

Shaking my head, I reached into my vest. "Here goes nothing."

I pulled the stone from my pocket and held it flat in my hand. It was cold to the touch, colder than it should have been since it had been pressed against me, but otherwise, completely normal. Arun and I both stared down at it, then at each other.

"Well?" he asked.

Estrid was peering over my shoulder. "What's supposed to happen?"

I didn't actually know. "I'm not sure, but I expect *something* is supposed to happen."

"Someone gives you a magic rock and you don't even ask how it works?" This from Erik who was hanging back, feigning disinterest in the proceedings, but apparently unable to keep his opinions to himself.

"It's magic," I said with a shrug. "How was I supposed to even know what to ask?" Despite my bravado, I had a sinking feeling in my chest. I'd wanted nothing more than for them to listen to me, and now that they were, I had absolutely nothing to tell them.

# CHAPTER 22

She was dead.

That was the only explanation.

I paced back and forth on the deck, ignoring the others' suggestions.

The star on my eye told me I was the right person. Raven's story told me I was bound to the heir whether I liked it or not. So, the only reason the rock wouldn't guide me to her would be if she no longer existed.

Right?

But wouldn't I know if she were dead? Would our bond tell me that?

Then again, I hadn't even known I was bound to anyone until the day before.

"I need a heading," Arun called eventually as I made another circuit around the deck.

"Well, I don't have one for you." The rock was still cold in my hand, although my hands were sweating with nerves. Strange, but not helpful. I stared down at it, willing it to do something— anything at all.

"Um, Frida?"

"I told you," I said irritably, "I don't know yet."

"No, that's not it."

I looked up to find him pointing toward the west where the sun was sinking. Squinting into the horizon, I saw dozens of flying objects growing closer. "What is it?" I stashed the rock back inside my vest to be safe.

"Looks like—"

"Ur'gels!" Erik ran toward the rear of the ship, sword already drawn.

But it wasn't just ur'gels. Leading the pack, flying faster than I'd ever seen her fly, was Stiarna. The ur'gels snapped at her wings and her rear legs, and she was whirling and diving and pushing herself forward. She must have been hunting when they found her, and she'd brought them right to us in her panic.

She crashed to the deck in a pile of wings and claws, and my ax cut cleanly through the neck of the ur'gel who had been hot on her heels. His body went one way and his head went the other, rolling to a stop at Stiarna's feet. She plucked it up in her beak and tossed it over the side of the ship. Then, seeming to recover her bravery, she took off into the air again, chasing after another ur'gel who zoomed past us.

The other ur'gels congregated around the ship like buzzards circling their prey. Some of them carried non-fliers and dropped them to the deck. A particularly large one ran at me, his protruding incisors turning his smile into a grimace. When my sword hit his arm, instead of slicing through it, the skin deflected it like armor.

That was new.

It laughed, wrapped its iron hand around the blade, and jerked it from me, tossing it aside. My ax was in my other hand, but I didn't want to lose it, too, so I dropped it into my belt. The ur'gel swung at me and I ducked, over and over until we were pressed against the railing. It took another swing and I went to my back, braced my feet on its stomach, and using its own momentum, propelled it up and over the side.

I scrambled to my feet, grabbing the railing and leaning over to watch it fall. And fall it did, fast and hard, like a stone. A flier went after it, but I didn't think it stood much of a chance of catching it before it crashed to the ground.

Turning back, I surveyed the others. Erik had gathered up a rope and was using it as a lasso, pulling fliers to the deck where Estrid waited to dispatch them. Arun was using his bow. I watched an arrow tear a hole in a wing, and the flier spin wildly out of control, dropping below the ship and out of view. He was quickly out of arrows, though, and turned his attention back to the wheel and keeping the ship under control. While I watched, though, his eyes went wide.

"What is it?" I asked, shouting over the din.

"The sheriu box." Arun was pointing up with one hand, the other white-knuckling the wheel to keep us on course.

I looked up to see a small, winged ur'gel examining the blue box at the top of the mainmast. Without hesitating, I ran for the rigging and began climbing the rope net that reached up to the first yardarm. It was a climb I'd made often, but never with any urgency. Trying to hurry made me careless and my feet got stuck in the nets, actually making the climb even slower.

When I reached the first yardarm, I scooted along it to the next net, and climbed even higher, keeping myself hidden by the white sails. All the while, I kept the ur'gel in my sights. It was fiddling with the box, trying to remove it from the mast. If he did that, I suspected we would plummet to the ground. Much as the armored ur'gel had done.

I made it to the third sail before the wind began to knock me around. I held on tight and continued my climb, my arms and legs trembling with the effort. The ur'gel hadn't seen me yet, but when it did. Well, I would deal with that when it came down to it.

Finally, I came over the top of the fourth and final sail and balanced on the yard arm, one hand on the narrow mast, my ax in the other. The ur'gel looked over its shoulder, saw me, and shrieked. I quieted it with an ax to the forehead. He released the box and fell, his wings whipping in the wind. He fell at Estrid's feet. She looked up, saw me, and saluted, before turning to face her next opponent, a flier with a nasty scar running across its face.

I was just contemplating how to get back down and re-enter the fight, when a sudden silence befell us. The fliers were gone, and the only ur'gels on the deck were dead ones.

"Where did they go?" I shouted down to my siblings.

Erik and Estrid each ran to one side of the ship, and when they looked back, glancing between me and Arun with wide eyes, I had a sickening feeling.

"Get down, Frida," Erik called. "Quick."

But Estrid was shaking her head. "There isn't time. Secure yourself."

What was she talking about? The ship trembled, and I hugged the mast, the wood scraping against my cheek.

Estrid tied a rope around a hook on the deck, and then wrapped the other end around her waist before going to Arun and helping him secure his hands to the wheel. Erik was doing the same, unfurling a length of rope and knotting it around his chest.

The ship heaved, tilting to one side. My feet slipped off the yardarm and I scrambled for purchase. That was when I understood. The ur'gels were below the ship. Not able to remove the box, they were going to take us down another way. They were going to capsize the *Duchess*. And if I didn't get myself secured, I would be going down with it.

But there were no loose ropes up here, nothing I could tie around myself or use as an anchor.

My time had run out. The ship rocked perilously. I wrapped

one of my hands in a rope connected to the sail and held on to the mast with the other. My feet came out from under me and we were sideways, nothing between me and the ground but hundreds of feet of air. I heard someone screaming but I couldn't focus on anything except not letting go.

The ship groaned again. Crates and boxes slid off the deck and I watched them fall, disappearing before they exploded against the ground. My hand burned, the fingers turning blue, but I would not let go.

"Hang on!" someone shouted, maybe Arun.

We kept going, kept turning, and then my feet were dangling past the sheriu box which should have been over my head. The trees and the rocks and the winding river below me were so far away they seemed like child's toys, like I could pick them up and move them around at my will. My hand slipped, my arm tingling as the rope cut off the blood supply.

But I would not let go. I tried to fold my feet underneath me, to find something to grab onto, but there was nothing. Suddenly, there was a creaking, a snap, and the rope—

I was falling.

The rope had broken, snapped under my weight.

I screamed. Something rushed at me. An ur'gel, I thought, coming to finish the job. I tried to free my ax, but it was impossible as I fell, twisting and turning in the air.

And then something tugged the back of my shirt and jerked me to a stop.

I rose again, my stomach flip-flopping at the sudden change. I looked up to see Stiarna, her front talons wrapped in my shirt. She pulled me close to her and I climbed over her shoulder until I was on her back, one leg on each side of her, tucked just below her wings.

Leaning low, I patted her neck. "Let's get them."

We approached the deck of the ship, where Estrid and Erik and Arun were doing a better job at holding on than I'd done.

Stiarna pulled up alongside Arun, who was flat against the wheel, his face pale and his teeth grinding together.

"Get them off the ship," he managed to say. "Get them off and she'll right herself."

I nodded, and we came out from under the deck and moved past the railing. The bottom of the ship—which was now the top—was covered with whatever ur'gels were left, all of them happily resting on their haunches while they waited for us to die. I was glad they were too stupid to think to finish us off while we were dangling helplessly over the ground.

Stiarna hit them at full speed, scattering several of them who fluttered away with howling protests. We wheeled around and came back at them again. This time, I had my ax. I cut down two of them as we passed, Stiarna using her powerful rear claws against another. The ur'gels seemed too stunned to launch much of a defense, and we made three passes at them before the ship began to roll back into place. Some of them made a final, valiant attempt, standing their ground on the bottom of the ship. Stiarna dove at one, snatching him with her talons and tossing him overboard. The others quickly gave up after that, scattering to the wind, flapping away as fast as their wings could carry them.

The *Iron Duchess* righted herself quickly when their weight was gone. Stiarna waited for it to stop rocking before touching down in front of Arun, who was on his knees, untying his hands with trembling fingers.

Erik freed himself and rushed to the side, where he retched loudly over the railing. Estrid and I looked at each other and cringed, and then I turned to Arun.

"They'll be back," I told him. "Probably with reinforcements. We have to do something."

I knew what I wanted to do. I wanted to get down. I wanted to get out of the air and plant my feet on solid, unmoving ground. I was done with flying.

"We have to go up," Arun said finally, color returning to his cheeks as he righted himself. "We're near Lamruil. If we can get higher, past the veil, we can get help."

Right. Of course.

Up it was, then.

# CHAPTER 23

We didn't have much of a respite from the onslaught of ur'gels. They came back before we'd broken through the veil, and this time, they were being more careful about it. They stayed off the deck and out of reach of our weapons. Instead, they dangled off the hull nets and perched on the masts, doing their best to weigh the ship down.

"What kind of help will Lamruil offer?" I asked Arun. From what I knew of the High Elves, they were good fighters, but not quick to join any fight that wasn't theirs.

He was tugging on the lever, urging his ship higher. She was fighting him with every foot she climbed. "If we can get there, we can enlist the help of the High Elves living there to fight off the ur'gels. They don't want these creatures there any more than we want them on our ship."

So, we would make it their fight, then.

"I can't get us there, though, not with all this weight on the ship."

I looked at my siblings. "Are you guys up for another fight?"

Estrid slid her swords from their sheaths. "Always. I'll take the ones on the masts."

Knocking his own sword against his shield, Erik said, "Send them down to me on the deck."

Arun nodded at me. "That leaves you and Stiarna the hull nets."

"No problem," I nodded, looking at the gryphon on the deck, the thought of flying on anything making me queasy, but especially her made it worse.

Stiarna stretched her wings wide readying herself for battle. Quickly, I jumped on her back, locking my knees tight around her sides. Exhaling, she launched over the side rail of the *Duchess* and towards the hull nets.

Directly below us, more than a dozen flying ur'gel climbed up the nets, pulling the splintered wood from the side of the *Duchess*. Almost like they were attempting to claw their way into the bowels of the boat. If any of them found a pathway through they could easily get to the main deck where Eric and Estrid were focused on taking down their own assemblage of ur'gels.

"We've got this Stiarna." I patted her golden feathers at her neck. "Let's work our way from top to bottom."

I eyed a leathery winged ur'gel at the top of the hull nets as I let my ax fall from my belt and into my right hand. Stiarna made a beeline for the ur'gel just as his oily hand reached the top rung. My ax sliced through the back of his head, spraying black blood all over Stiarna's golden coat. The ur'gel toppled over, taking another ur'gel with him as he plummeted to the ground below.

The remaining ur'gels turned their attention to Stiarna and I as their fallen comrades crashed through the trees. Pushing off the side of the *Duchess*, the ur'gel took flight. I dug my fingers further into Stiarna's neck as she whipped around flapping her massive wings towards the stern of the boat.

"Now what?" I peeked over my shoulder.

Stiarna clucked at me in frustration. If she were human, I could picture her rolling her eyes at me.

I grimaced as I watched Estrid lithely climb the masts and start dispatching ur'gels, sending dead and alive alike to Erik, who quickly threw their bodies overboard.

Stiarna shook her massive head and squealed with what I could only describe as glee as she soared in a circle to gather speed as I squeezed my eyes shut to avoid looking at the ground again. I had known if I never flew again it would be too soon.

As she righted herself, I opened my eyes and looked at the mess below the hull and contemplated how to get rid of this many ur'gels without killing myself at the same time.

Screams sounded from above as an ur'gel with shredded wings flew past me, his friends in the net watching him fall.

"If you don't want to end up like him, you can just fly away."

A small shuffling of wings, a scratching of a stomach, and a roar of laughter was my answer.

Great.

Squeezing Stiarna behind the wings, I edged her forward, slashing at one ur'gel while she grabbed another and ripped holes in his wings.

Nothing from the ur'gels sitting in the nets. It was almost as if they were being controlled by some invisible force to stay there. To sacrifice themselves. No matter, they had to move so we could fly, not just float. Another pass, two more ur'gels. I paused, listening for the fighting on the deck, but it seemed just as dulled as here.

Taking control, I led Stiarna back above the hull and hovered, watching my siblings work to clear the masts, Arun holding the ship steady.

"What are you doing up here? Have you cleared them out from below already?" his voice cut across the air.

"No, haven't you noticed the lack of resistance to fighting?

Almost as though they are drugged or something?" I asked them.

"Who cares as long as we get them off the ship?" Erik shouted at me from the deck.

"I don't know. What if it's a trap? What if there's something worse? Bigger?" I couldn't stop thinking this was too easy.

"Get rid of the ur'gels in the hull netting or I'll show you a trap." Arun shouted at me as he slightly adjusted course, glaring over the wheel of the ship. Sighing I ducked back down to the hull, the ur'gels staring at me.

"I was hoping you wouldn't figure it out, heir." A voice came from behind me. I rolled my eyes and turned.

"Am not. For the last time."

"We shall see. I have no need to stay and watch the fight, you will come to me. I hope you enjoy the fight. There are plenty more of these." I watched as she disappeared again, and heard the growling start behind me, the ur'gels waking from their trances.

Spinning, Stiarna lunged at the one nearest her, while I cleaved the one nearest me, his head flying to the trees below, blood splattering his neighbor. We dodged and weaved as the ship rose slightly. Each body that flew from above, dead and alive, had wings torn so they couldn't catch flight, helping the ship gain slightly more air.

I could hear Erik and Estrid calling to one another, though not what they were saying as bodies hit the deck, shrieking as they were thrown into the sky with no way to save themselves. A small, tight smile graced my lips as I slashed and hacked at the ur'gels here, Stiarna crunching on their heads, wings, anything she could get her beak or claws on.

Taunting them, I tried to get as many as I could to chase us around the ship, flying low through the deck so Erik could hit them with his shield, or Estrid could slash their wings if they wouldn't go low. If they wouldn't chase us, I just slashed their wings.

Stiarna squawked in joy every time she tore into another ur'gel, racing faster before floating slowly to taunt them, my unease at flying forgotten for the time being.

Finally, almost all the ur'gels were either dead or trying to escape the netting on the hull, and tangling themselves more as they squirmed, making themselves easy to pick off, before tearing the corpses out of the net and dropping them like weighted stones to the surface below.

An ur'gel sans head fell from above nearly missing Stiarna and me just as we veered right around the rudder. Its head followed, knocking out the ur'gel closest to us. In shock, that one plunged to the ground. More black blood sprayed around us as another part of an ur'gel fell from above.

I'd have to remember to thank my siblings for the flying ur'gel parts later.

One of the smaller, but faster ur'gels flew next to us. His sharp claws grabbed at Stiarna's wing, tipping us sideways. My grip loosened as Stiarna dove below the boat, the ur'gel giving chase.

Falling to my death was not what I had planned for the day. We needed to get out of the air sooner not later. But no, Arun insisted we go higher.

Stiarna leveled us back up next to the hull nets just as the ur'gel crashed into us from behind. My already loosened fingers lost purchase and I tipped backwards off of Stiarna.

Grabbing on to the last rung of the net I hefted myself up with my ax in hand. The butt of my ax rammed into the forehead of an approaching ur'gel as the blade sliced through its guts, leaving just two ur'gels for us to finish off.

In horror, a thin ur'gel began to crawl through a hole in the *Duchess*. Its wings buzzed and legs stuck out like a bee squirming its way into a hive. Throwing my ax, I sliced through his wings as a howl left the ur'gel. Thankfully, my ax plunged itself into the side of the boat, we did not have time for an added mission of finding my loss ax. The ur'gel slid out of the hole and fell to his death below.

One left.

My eyes went to where I had last seen the ur'gel. It was gone.

"Frida." Estrid called from above as her head poked over the rail.

My eyes glanced up taking in my blood coated sister, sword in hand. A wide smile spread across her face. "We got them all" she called down.

"One more," I muttered to myself. Of course, they'd finished off their batch before me.

"Stiarna," I called as I pulled my ax out of the side of the boat, scattering splintered wood around me. I needed to get into the air and find this ur'gel.

A loud bang behind me had me twisting around just as the last ur'gel went to plunge his sharp claw through my back.

Stiarna ripped it from the net, tore a huge gash in its wing, and the last ur'gel fell. Beside us, the ship finally began to rise.

The deck was painted black with ur'gel blood, but everything else seemed "simply cosmetic" as Arun would say. They would be back, and stronger in number, but one thing was sure…

I was so over flying.

# CHAPTER 24

The veil parted around us, the white moisture from the clouds rolling around the masts and off the deck like smoke. The sun had nearly gone down now, but we weren't met with darkness. Instead, the blue light of Gleet shone on a luminous city of green gardens and glass towers. The winding streets of the plateau were lit with the familiar yellow light of yooperlite stones. Arun had told me the elves used them, but I had never imagined anything quite like this.

It wasn't just what was on the plateau that caught my attention, but also what was around it. Dozens of airships like the *Iron Duchess* hovered around the island, some docked at what I guessed were air docks, while others floated lazily just offshore, their decks lit with yooperlite and revealing elven crews.

In comparison to the serenity of Lamruil, we were like a blazetaur crashing the party, with our skeleton crew and a band of angry and determined ur'gels on our tail. I could feel eyes on us and knew the moment the ur'gels burst through the veil as well before I even turned around, based on the reaction of elves on other ships. They grabbed their weapons and rushed to their positions, ready to beat a quick retreat.

Arun was digging around in a box beneath the wheel and came out with a red bit of cloth that he handed to Erik. "Run this up the mainmast. Quick."

"What is it?" I asked.

"A distress flag."

On cue, an ur'gel landed in Erik's path and jerked the red flag from his hand, tossing it aside. Erik drew up short, surprised, and the ur'gel got in a lucky strike, its nails slicing three cuts in the front of Erik's shirt. I moved forward but Estrid was already there, reaching over Erik's shoulder and plunging a sword into the ur'gel's forehead.

"You're bleeding," she said to Erik.

Erik looked down at himself. "Mere scratches." And then he dropped to his knees and toppled over.

Estrid and I knelt beside him. There were three long gashes in his shirt. She pulled the shirt away, ripping it and revealing deep, jagged wounds beneath. Three of them, one of them flashing white bone beneath. I pressed a hand to my mouth.

"The flag," Estrid said.

I nodded and stood, recovering the flag, and running it up the rope on the mainmast. It was a clear call to action. As soon as it was up, other ships began to move toward us instead of away. Captains shouted inaudible orders at their crews. Men could be seen running back and forth, pulling on ropes, and releasing sails, turning their airships in our direction.

Estrid was pressing strips of torn shirt to Erik's wounds. I longed for Aria, who would have been able to stitch his skin back together. Even for Beru or Ravyn, who would help us fight these monsters.

"Go," Estrid said. "Help Arun."

I was hesitant to leave Erik but saw what Estrid meant. Another ship was drawing up alongside the *Duchess*, and Arun was trying to keep her steady while fighting off an ur'gel who was hovering over his head. As I ran toward him, I threw my ax and sent the ur'gel tumbling to the deck.

It landed on its feet, though, and more were coming. Stiarna swiped one out of the sky and pressed its throat between the sharp points of her beak. Estrid stood over Erik's body and fended off two more who were playing with her, lunging one at a time and circling. Still others surged over the railing and shimmied down the masts. They couldn't defeat us in battle, so it seemed their strategy would be just to wear us down.

I slid to a stop, retrieved my ax from where it had fallen, and spun, swinging it in a wide arc at the nearest ur'gel. It grazed his chest from shoulder to shoulder, but the cut was superficial. I was panting. The ur'gel lunged but I was slow to react, sluggish and exhausted for no reason. It threw me across the deck and I crashed into another body. Arms wrapped around my waist and kept me upright. I turned around to see a man in a three-corner hat looking up at me. His ears were tapered to points like Arun's, marking him as a High Elf. He had a long sword at one hip, and a galestone pistol at the other.

"It's the air up here," he said in a rough, unfamiliar voice.

"What?"

"The air is thinner. You're used to the pressure below the veil. If you haven't lived up here your whole life, it will affect your performance drastically."

That explained the sluggishness and the fact that the ur'gel had gotten a hit in. It was a monster designed for battle, I was not. I was a D'ahvol, true, but still not a monster, despite what some people thought.

Beyond the man's shoulder, I saw a ship and sailors swinging across from it to ours, landing and joining the growing battle on our decks. Other sailors lined the ship's railing and loosed arrows into the ur'gels who were hovering around the *Duchess*. There was another ship on our other side doing the same. The man who'd been talking to me tipped his hat, then raised his sword and gave a deep yell before diving into the fray.

I surveyed the fight, looking for somewhere to jump in. Arun looked like he was having a blast, but Estrid was still alone, defending Erik who had pushed himself to a sitting position against the railing and was swinging a sword at anything that came to near. Crossing to them, I nodded at Estrid and took my position at her back. I'd seen her and Erik fight like this countless times, and now it was my turn.

It felt nice to have someone behind me. It left me free to focus all my attention on the ur'gels coming at me and Erik from the front. Two of them came at me at once and I pushed them back easily, taking a few steps away from Erik as I did.

Estrid reached back and grabbed me. "What are you doing?" she snapped. "Never leave your partner unguarded." Her tone was sharp and unforgiving. Mean. Like it had been whenever Savarah was around.

I felt it too. The urge to snap back at her. To turn my ax on her. Instead of doing either of those things, I looked around and saw elf turning on elf, fighting over trivial things, like who had stepped on whose toes. I watched one pair arguing over whose turn it was to kill an ur'gel when that very ur'gel drove its claws through their chests, lifting them off the deck and tossing them overboard.

Something was wrong.

A flash of gold caught my eye. I turned to the bow and watched as a large, winged ur'gel appeared, a towheaded woman in a deep red dress in its arms, her hands laced around its meaty neck.

Savarah.

The ur'gel placed her on the bow and she walked forward as if she owned the place, unnoticed by anyone but me. She raised her hands in the air, palms out, and the fighting around us died as everyone—elf and ur'gel—turned to look at her. How had we missed it before, her ability to manipulate people? It was so obvious now.

She stopped a few yards from us and looked from me to Estrid, and then down to Erik, who was breathing hard, a hand on the wound in his chest.

"Erik, darling." Her voice was like honey, smooth and rich. "Give me Frida and I will let the rest of you go free. I'll even heal those nasty scratches before you go."

I turned to Erik, ready to stop him. Ready to defend myself if he went after me.

But he just smiled. It was a weak smile, but still a smile. And he said, "Not a chance, Savarah. We know who you are, but you forget who we are."

She put her hands on her hips, eyebrows raised, clearly not used to being defied. "And who is that, exactly?"

He looked away from her and nodded at me. "We're D'ahvol."

That was all I needed to hear. I rushed Savarah while everyone else was still frozen under her spell. She screamed, and that scream released them, but it was too late. I was already on top of her. She had her throwing knives in her hand, but they were small, feeling like insignificant pinpricks on my arms as I shoved her back. Pressing her to the railing, I grabbed her wrists and squeezed until the knives fell from her hands.

"Frida, stop," she said in a voice that was used to being obeyed.

But not by me. Without an ounce of mercy, I took her by the shoulders and threw her over the side of the ship. The ur'gels who were left on the *Duchess* took off after her, swooping down and disappearing below the veil. Maybe they would save her, maybe they wouldn't. One thing was for certain, though.

Savarah would never again be able to control the Svand siblings.

# CHAPTER 25

The other sailors returned to their airships, some of them carrying bodies, others mourning the loss of bodies not found. Soon we were alone again on the *Iron Duchess*, just the four of us. For once, we were able to breathe.

With the ship hovering and not in any danger, Arun was walking around, taking stock of anything that had been broken. With every new bit of damage he found, he would say her name in a low, apologetic voice and rub her lovingly. I wasn't sure what the big deal was, though. The railing was smashed in several places, and one of the masts had been knocked askew, splintering slightly beneath the first sail. Other than that, and scratches in the wood paneling and blood stains on the deck, she was largely intact.

The same could also be said for Erik. The bleeding had stopped in all but one scratch, and Arun assured us the medics on Lamruil would be able to sew it up and give him something to prevent infection. Estrid had him on his feet and together, we watched Arun make his rounds, lamenting the damage done to his ship.

When he finished his rounds and returned to the helm, I followed.

He seemed quiet, thoughtful, as he took the wheel and began to guide us toward the city. Stiarna was beside him. He rubbed his fingers through the fur on her back. She purred loudly, the strumpet.

I leaned against the railing beside him and broke the silence between us with a question. "Are you excited to return?" What I really wanted to know was if this was where we parted. If this was the end of his time with us. With me. Would he go back and marry Tsarra? Settle down on his estate? Sell the *Duchess*?

He looked at me like I was crazy. "Certainly not. But we'll have to stay for a time to repair the *Duchess* before continuing our quest."

"You could, you know ... stay here. Go home. If you wanted."

He glanced over at me, his face changing from serious to playful. "Are you trying to get rid of me, Svand?"

I didn't want him to leave, but it seemed only fair to give him a way out if he wanted one. "No, I'm just saying."

"Do you want me to go?"

This time it was my turn to be serious. I put a hand on the wheel just beside his. "No."

He placed his hand over mine and squeezed. It was warm, rough, and comforting. "Then I'm not going anywhere."

"What if I can't find the heir? How long will you search with me? How long before my lost cause isn't fun anymore?"

"There's no time limit." He smiled again. "But I believe you'll find her. I believe you'll save the world, even if you don't want to."

I didn't like the blush that rose in my cheeks, so instead of responding, I wandered away to the back of the ship. The sky was completely black now, and the stars had come out, the small lights of my ancestors winking down at me. I wondered if my mother was up there, and if she was glad I finally knew the truth. That she had fought for me until the very end.

*Never forget to look up,* my father had said.

And so, I did.

Arun eased the ship into a slip at an air dock, barely bumping against the sides. I put one of Erik's arms around my shoulders and Estrid took the other. We disembarked single file, Arun in front and Stiarna bringing up the rear.

But we didn't get halfway down the dock before another group was walking toward us. Their leader was a woman in a tricorn hat with curly black hair and more weapons strapped to her than I could count. I itched to draw my ax but knew that would only cause trouble. She was flanked by two elves who seemed to be in some sort of uniform—red jackets and black slacks, with long swords slung over their shoulders.

Our two groups met in the middle of the walkway and stopped.

"I am Captain Wynleth of the *Wind Wraith,*" the woman said in introduction. She looked down her nose at us, clearly finding us barely deserving of her attentions. "The high king requests your presence."

Part of me wanted to fight back, to argue with her. But looking around, I knew we were done fighting, at least for now. I nodded at Arun, who had looked back at me. He, in turn, nodded to the woman, motioning for her to lead the way.

Our motley crew followed—three D'ahvol, a High Elf, and a griffin—ready to face whatever the next step was on our journey to find the Suun heir.

Continue reading this series, Legends of the Fallen with book 6, Finding the Suun

Grab the free prequel to the Legends of the Fallen series, Falling Suun here:
https://books2read.com/u/3R1ElD

Like the series Facebook page to stay up to date on all new releases
https://www.facebook.com/LegendsoftheFallen

# ABOUT THE AUTHOR

J.A. Culican is a USA Today Bestselling author of the middle grade fantasy series Keeper of Dragons. Her first novel in the fictional series catapulted a trajectory of titles and awards, including top selling author on the USA Today bestsellers list and Amazon, and a rightfully earned spot as an international best seller. Additional accolades include Best Fantasy Book of 2016, Runner-up in Reality Bites Book Awards, and 1st place for Best Coming of Age Book from the Indie Book Awards.

J.A. Culican holds a master's degree in Special Education from Niagara University, in which she has been teaching special education for over 13 years. She is also the president of the autism awareness non-profit Puzzle Peace United. J.A. Culican resides in Southern New Jersey with her husband and four young children.

For more information about J.A. Culican, visit her website at: www.jaculican.com.

# ABOUT THE AUTHOR

Cassidy studied English and Creative Writing at the University of North Carolina at Chapel Hill and won the Bill Hooks Award for Young Adult Fiction in 2007. She lives in beautiful North Carolina with her husband, two kids, two dogs, and one cat who thinks he's a dog.

For more information about Cassidy Taylor, visit her website at: http://cassidytaylor.net/

# ACKNOWLEDGMENTS

Editor: Frankie Blooding
Cover Artist: Christian Bentulan
Formatting: Dragon Realm Press

9 781949 621112